CW00517337

WARDTOWN

A *TEXAS RANGER* Novel

BRAD DENNISON

Author of THE LONG TRAIL and
WANDERING MAN

Wardtown is a work of fiction. Names, characters, places, and incidents are either the product of the author's imagination or are used fictitiously. Any resemblance to actual persons, living or dead, events or locales is entirely coincidental.

Copyright 2014 by Bradley A. Dennison.

Substantive Editors: Donna Dennison and Martha Gulick

Cover Design: Donna Dennison

Copy Editor: Loretta Yike

To My Family,

They make living with a writer look easy.

A special thanks to Leon Shook. It was during a phone call with him that he asked me to write this book. Without that phone call, this book probably wouldn't exist.

PART ONE
THE GALLOWS

1

WE HAD an open-and-shut case against Jonathan Hooper, and it seemed to me such a case shouldn't take more than a couple of weeks. The witnesses testify, the jury makes the obvious decision, and then the judge delivers the sentence.

But it turned out Hooper had been socking away money in an account back east, something none of us knew about. He was able to afford a good lawyer who was able to arrange delay after delay.

And then jury selection took weeks, because it was difficult to find anyone who was impartial. Word of what had been going on in Wardtown reached far. Hooper had a reputation as "The Hanging Judge," even though he had been a judge by self-appointment only. Stories, some true and some not so true, had been reaching from the Panhandle to the Rio Grande. Eventually the trial had to be moved to a different county, and finally after juror selection was finished, the trial began to proceed.

I was called in for testimony and cross examination that lasted two full days. Sam Wilson had to take the stand, and he was there most of a day. At one point it looked like the prosecution might want to call Maddie Shannon to the stand, but she had left for St. Louis months earlier and hadn't been heard from.

I thought if she was needed for testimony at least I would get to see her again. I have to admit, my heart beat a little faster at the thought. But the prosecutor thought maybe she had been through enough and decided he would hold off sending for her unless it was absolutely necessary.

Joe McCabe had come along, too. I had asked the prosecutor not to call him to the stand unless it was absolutely necessary. He asked for a reason and I said I would give it if it was necessary for the case, but not until then.

The truth was, Joe McCabe was going by the name Smith, and didn't want anyone to know who he really was. Wilson and I were two of the few who knew. Joe was running from something—he had never told me what it was, and it wasn't the way of men of the west to ask. We just accepted what a man said and let it go at that.

Once Sam and I were no longer needed for testimony, we headed back to Wardtown. After all, I was the town marshal and Sam had a ranch to run.

It was the morning of February 22nd that I got the telegram from the prosecuting attorney. A telegraph wire had been strung into town after Hooper's reign had ended. Hooper had indeed been found guilty on fifteen counts of murder and numerous other counts charges such as larceny and kidnapping. Despite all of the money he had poured into buying a high-brow lawyer, he was to be hanged by the neck until dead.

I was standing on the boardwalk in front of the telegraph office, holding the telegram with one hand and a tin cup filled with coffee in the other. In the months since Hooper had been arrested, Wardtown had become so downright peaceful that I often walked my morning rounds with a cup of coffee. Joe joked that if I happened across a troublemaker, I could subdue him by throwing hot coffee in his face.

Joe was standing beside me as I read the telegram. Wilson was there, too.

"They're gonna hang him," I said to them as I read.

Sam had a lined face and a thick, gray mustache. His jaw was covered with scraggly whiskers, and he wore a tattered brown stetson.

He gave a sort of shrugging nod at what I had said. "No surprise there."

I stared at the telegram in silence.

Joe said, "What's wrong?"

"They're gonna stage it here."

Joe said, "Here?"

I nodded. "Seems it would be more justice for him to be executed in front of the people he had wronged."

Wilson nodded. "That's the way it's usually done with hangin's."

I nodded again but didn't say anything.

"What's wrong?" Joe said.

"I guess it was just that I was hoping we had seen the last of him. This town has put the Hooper years behind it. It's like it's turned a new page."

Wilson said, "When is the hanging scheduled?"

"A couple weeks from now. The prosecutor tried to petition the judge to give us a little time to prepare for it."

"Two weeks ain't a whole lot of time to

prepare. Not for someone like Hooper."

"They're bringing the prisoner here next week."

Joe said, "Jonathan Hooper. Here in our jail."

"If that's not a prescription for trouble," Wilson said, "I don't know what is."

I looked at Joe. "I'm gonna need you full time, until this is over."

Wilson said, "I can spare him."

"All right," Joe said. "You've got yourself a full-time deputy."

2

SAM WILSON SENT some men out from the ranch and we shored up the brick walls in the jail. We made sure the wrought iron bars in the window and the door to the cell were solid. The last thing I wanted was our prisoner escaping.

I had gone to the town leaders requesting additional money so I could pay Joe a full-time wage. Originally, all they could manage to squeeze out of their town budget was a few dollars so Joe could work part-time. Now, however, the business leaders in our little town dug deep and produced enough money to not only pay Joe, but to hire a third, at least until this was over. There was a young cowhand by the name of Will Church who worked for Sam, and he had some experience working as a shotgun rider for a stage company, and he had served as a deputy once out in New Mexico territory. Wilson turned him over to me.

It was on the morning of March second that we heard the unmistakable rumble of horse hooves and the rattle of a wagon. It began dimly at first, but then began to grow louder. I was standing in front of the jail, a little too antsy with anticipation to sit and do the paperwork I should have been doing. Joe was out there with me, pacing about with a hand-rolled smoke.

Wilson was here, too. He had ridden in this morning. He had said he wouldn't miss this for the world. He also thought I might need another gun hand in case someone decided to take it upon themselves to execute Hooper before his hanging date.

A young kid came running. He was maybe ten, and I knew him only as Billy. His face might have been freckled—I couldn't tell because it was always dirty. He was in ovralls and was barefoot, and was calling out, "They're comin'! They're comin'!"

People emerged from buildings to stand on the boardwalk. This was an event people didn't want to miss. The return of the notorious Jonathan Hooper. You would have thought it was Jesse James himself coming to visit our little jail.

Most of the people here had never actually seen Hooper. They had moved in after Joe and I arrested him and broke up his little army of gunfighters. Their knowledge of Hooper came from only what they had read, or heard word-of-mouth.

This was the irony of staging the hanging here. Most of the people who had actually suffered under Hooper had scattered to the winds. Like Maddie.

Will Church was walking the rounds, a shotgun cradled in one arm, but at the sound of Billy calling, he turned around on the boardwalk and headed back to the jail.

We all stood watching as the procession came into view. The riders and the wagon. By now fifty people had lined the boardwalks. Not all were residents. Some were ranchers who had come in. Most of the hands from the Shannon ranch were here, and the hands from the old Brimley place had ridden in, too.

Four mounted Texas Rangers led the procession. Following them was a stagecoach, and behind them were four more. This was an unusually large group of men for transporting only one prisoner, but the prisoner was Jonathan Hooper. No one was taking any chances.

They reined up in front of the jail. One of the riders had   longish blonde hair and a tall hat, and two revolvers turned backward for a crossdraw. His name was Ike Hawkins. I knew him from my time riding with the Rangers.

He swung out of the saddle and extended a hand, which I shook.

He said, "Mornin', Tremain."

I nodded. "Hawkins."

"Got me a prisoner to deliver."

I nodded again. "So I see."

"All right," he called back. "Bring him in."

All the riders dismounted, and then one of them opened the stage door and Hooper stepped out.

He looked like the Hooper I remembered, except he had lost some weight. I suppose jail food can do that to you. He was in a jacket and tie, and wore no hat. His wrists were cuffed in front of him.

He glanced about the town quickly with eyes that always struck me as being a strange sort of icy blue. He then let his gaze settle on me, and he started to smile.

"Tremain," he said. He then looked at Joe and said, "And the man called Smith."

"Shut up," Hawkins said to him.

Hooper gave him an almost theatrical bow.

"Follow me," I said to Hawkins and stepped into the jail.

Hawkins followed, along with the prisoner.

My office was quite small and within less than a minute it was filled with Texas Rangers. Hooper held out his hands while Hawkins removed the cuffs.

Hooper glanced about my little office. "I love what you've done with the place."

"Shut your mouth," Hawkins said, "or I'll shut it for you."

Hooper gave him a glance. I saw some amusement in Hooper's eye, and also a little anger. It struck me then that no matter what emotion Hooper seemed to be showing, there was always an undercurrent of anger.

I held open the door to our only cell. Hooper again gave a theatrical bow, and stepped in. I swung the door shut and then turned the key to lock it and dropped the key into my shirt pocket.

Hooper said to me, "So, is there a chance you could arrange a visit from the lovely Miss Shannon? I would so appreciate a chance to see her again."

I said nothing to him. He apparently didn't know Maddie had left town, and even if she hadn't, I'm sure she wouldn't have wanted to see him. Except to maybe put a bullet in him.

I followed Hawkins out to the boardwalk. A crowd of people had advanced to stand in front of the jail.

"You're gonna have a problem," Hawkins said. "If it was anyone but you in charge here, I'd lay odds the prisoner doesn't live the night."

"He'll live," I said. "I won't stand for any lynching in my town."

He nodded. "You want me and some of the boys to stay? Captain McNelly gave us permission to, if you need us."

"No," I said. "We've got things well in hand. But thanks."

"Well, then, we got a long ride back." He held out his hand again and I gave it another shake. "Good luck, Tremain."

I grinned. "Don't need luck if you're good at what you do."

Hawkins returned the grin and then called out to his men, "Mount up!"

Joe and Sam and I stood and watched as they rode away. The crowd of people parted to let them through.

I then said to the crowd, "All right, you've seen what you came to see. Go on about your business."

They stood for a few moments, then began drifting away.

Joe said to me, "You don't like hangin's, do you? You've been downright out-of-sorts for days."

"What I don't like is when everyone gets all festive about it. Even with someone like Hooper, it's still a man's life that's being taken. Such a thing should never be celebrated."

"My brother has his late wife's aunt living with him. Or at least he did the last time I knew. She helped with the raising of the children after their mother died. She was a very literate woman. Frowned at you if you said *ain't*. She had a term to explain the huge crowds a public hangin' will draw. She called it *morbid curiosity*. Kind of a mouthful, but I think it hits the nail on the head."

"It's also hard having Hooper here in our jail.

Having to guard him, to keep him from being lynched, when in fact we'd like to be the first to string him up."

Joe nodded. "There is that."

3

THE OLD MOSSYHORN SALOON HAD BEEN
burned only days after Hooper's arrest. The way it
had been situated, it had sort of blocked the street at
the far end of town, so you had to ride around the
building if you were going to continue on out of
town. Sort of like the jail did at this end of the street.
The way the two buildings had been placed, you
could have stood outside the door to my office and
been facing the Mossyhorn at the other end of town.
But now the Mossyhorn was gone and there was just
an open space at the far end of the street. The charred
remains of the timbers and boards had been carted off
and now, months later, there was no indication that a
building had ever been there at all.

A new saloon had opened up in the building
that had been the hotel. The hotel where I had been
involved in a shootout with some of Hooper's men
when I had first come to town. What had been the
lounge was now a barroom. A wall that had separated
the lounge from a backroom had been knocked down
to make a larger barroom, and the rooms upstairs
were now where some of the girls who worked the
barroom entertained their customers.

On a Friday night the saloon was usually filled
to bursting with cowhands. Not only from the
Shannon ranch and the old Brimley place, but there
were a couple of other ranches further out and
Wardtown was the only town within riding distance.

I could hear the ruckus from the saloon from
where I was sitting in my office. Customers shouting
and hooting it up. Sudden bursts of loud laughter.

Tonight it was loud even for a Friday night—I figured our prisoner brought in a larger crowd than usual.

I was at my desk with a cup of coffee going. The paperwork I had been putting off was still on my desk in front of me. Reward posters I had to go over before I decided which ones to post. A report I had to fill out regarding my office's expenses. But I was tired and decided I would put them off until tomorrow. Or the next day.

Joe was in here with me, sitting on the corner of my desk with a cup of coffee in one hand. Will Church had gone out to walk the rounds.

Hooper was standing behind the barred door maybe ten feet behind me.

He said, "So, Marshal. How long do you think it will be before the good townsfolk come bursting in to try and hang me?"

"Don't think they're going to," I said without looking at him. The less I had to look at this man, the better.

He said, "Then you're not a very good judge of human nature. And the ironic thing is, as much as you want to hang me yourself, you have to protect me from them. But protect me, you will. Because that's your job, and you have this obsessive sense of duty."

"You think you know me so well."

"Oh, I indeed know you all too well. So, tell me, how is Miss Shannon these days?"

Now my ire was up, and I turned to face him. "Don't mention her name. You don't have the right."

Hooper was smiling. "Now, now, Marshal. Have I somehow hit upon a tender nerve?"

He was playing me. I knew it, which made me

even angrier.

I said, "There's nothing I would like more than to go in there and pound you senseless."

"But you won't. It's your job to protect your prisoner."

"I have to keep you alive until hanging day. That's all I have to do. There's nothing to keep me from, say, beating the hell out of you because you attempted escape."

Joe said. "If he don't, I might."

Hooper continued smiling. "How's that gun hand doing?"

"Good enough to drive a fist into that smug face of your'n."

Hooper grew silent. Wise choice on his part. He didn't know my deputy's real name, but he knew Joe was a capable man. Hooper had actually tried to recruit him at one point. Truth was, if the legends of the McCabe brothers were even half true, then Joe McCabe was probably the most capable man I had ever met.

I heard a sudden staccato rhythm of boots on the boardwalk out front, and Billy came charging in. Dirt clinging to his face, and a tattered wide-brimmed hat askew on his head.

He said, "Marshal! They're talking lynching at the saloon. It started with only a couple, but now they're getting the whole place fired up."

"Where's Will?"

"He's at the saloon. He told me to come get you."

I got to my feet. I normally didn't wear my gun when I was at my desk, but I had decided to make an exception tonight. I drew it and checked the loads. I had only five cartridges in place, so I pulled a sixth from the loops on my gunbelt and thumbed it in.

I slapped the gun back into my holster.

Joe said, "Want me to come with you?"

I shook my head. "You stay here. Bar the door. Don't let anyone in."

I stepped out, and I could hear the two-by-four that served to bar the door sliding into place. I then crossed the dark street and stepped onto the boardwalk and on down to the saloon.

I found Will standing just inside the doorway, his scattergun in hand. He was a little younger than I was, with a thick mustache and hair that fell to his collar. A light colored stetson with a pencil-rolled brim.

Seven men were standing and facing him. Cowhands, though I didn't recognize all of them. Two I knew from the Shannon ranch. Three others worked out at the Brimley place.

More were at the bar and others were at tables. They were calling out and shouting. It was hard to make out all of the words because when this many men are shouting, it can turn into a roar. But I heard shouts of *get out of our way!* And, *we're gonna string him up!* And, *gonna go get us a rope!* There were also a few disparaging remarks about Will's mother and doubting his heritage.

Will was shouting back at them. "The first man to make a move at me gets both barrels of this here shotgun!"

They didn't see me until I stepped around Will to stand beside him. The room quieted all at once.

"Howdy, Stu," I said, to one of the cowhands from the Shannon Ranch.

"Marshal," he said, looking a little sheepish.

I looked at one of the cowhands from the Brimley ranch. "Perkins."

"Howdy, Marshal."

I then looked at the crowd. "You boys been making a lot of noise. But there's such a thing called law-and-order, and I'm the one paid to enforce it. Will and me, and Smith back at the jail. Jonathan Hooper has been tried in court and found guilty, and he'll hang. You got my word on that. But he'll hang on the appointed date. Four days from now. It'll be done all legal-like."

"Law and order?" One man called out from the back. "I'll give you law and order!"

Another shouted, "You know what you can do with your law-and—"

His words were cut off because the room broke out into a chaotic din again. More calls for getting a rope.

I drew my gun and fired into the ceiling. I did it fast and they weren't expecting it. The cowhands facing Will and me backed up a step. Even Will jumped.

"I don't want anyone hurt," I said. "But we're going to do this the right way, as required by law."

One man stepped forward. He was no cowhand. He had the look of a man who had been on the trail a while. His vest looked like it had once belonged to a three-piece-suit but was now dingy and tattered, and his shirt might have been white once, but now was a sort of brown and gray combination because of ground-in trail dust. His hat was covered with dust and sweat had soaked through the crown, and the brim had gone floppy. But his gun was worn low and tied down for a quick draw. A saddle tramp with dreams of being a gunfighter, and he was looking to create a name for himself. Apparently wanting to start here.

He said, "The only law I know is the law of my gun. Now we're gonna go hang a man, and we're gonna cut down anyone who gets in the way."

I said, "You really think you can get past me?"

He was smiling. He saw it as a challenge, even though my gun was already in my hand. He had some whiskey in him, and whiskey can bring on what I call *stupid courage*. The courage to do something dangerous and stupid, when common sense should call on you to back off and give it some more thought.

One man called out from somewhere in the crowd, "We don't need law and order! We need a rope!"

A deep baritone spoke from behind me. "We need law and order, gentleman, because if we don't have it, then we're no better than Jonathan Hooper himself."

I didn't take my eyes off the man with the tied-down gun. But I heard boot soles striking the floor behind me, and a man walked around from behind Will and me to stand beside us. He was my height, and in a black string tie and a dark, pin-striped jacket and a wide-brimmed hat. He had a black mustache and goatee. He stood strong, his shoulders filling out his jacket. At his right side was a revolver, holstered low and tied down.

Something about the way this man stood and the look in his eye, he wasn't any kind of pretender. His right thumb was hooked into his belt above the holster, only inches from the handle of his pistol, and I had the feeling he could have that gun out and firing fast enough.

He said to the man I was facing, "There's going to be no hanging tonight, my friend. The only man who's going to die is you, if you really mean to challenge the marshal."

The man looked from one of us to the other. He then took a reluctant step backward.

I said, "All of you, just settle on down. We don't want anyone hurt here tonight. Jonathan Hooper will hang, I assure you of that. But it will be done under the hand of the law."

Stu nodded, still looking sheepish. Some of the wind had been knocked out of his sails. He hit the man beside him in the shoulder and said, "Come on. Let's get out of here."

Men at the tables and the bar remained silent.

"Let's get back to the jail," I said to Will.

He and I stepped out, and the stranger followed us.

I said to him, "I owe you a word of thanks. My name's Austin Tremain."

He grinned. "I know who you are, Marshal. Your exploits here a few months ago are being talked about all the way north to Montana, believe me. And all the way east to Saint Louis. That's where I first heard it."

He extended his hand. "Doctor Thomas

Benson, M.D."

A doctor? I wasn't expecting this. I shook his hand.

"I just arrived in town a few minutes ago. I could have taken the stage, but I prefer to travel by horseback. I'm renting out some space above the feed store for an office."

We began walking toward the jail as we talked.

Will Church said, "You're not like any doctor I ever seen."

He shrugged. "I have a diverse background. I was an officer in the late War Between the States. I saw too many men die, so I decided to do something about it, and went to medical school. Now, here I am. I stepped in back there at the saloon because I didn't really want any customers my first night in town, and the way things were going, someone was going to get shot."

We reached the jail. I said, "Come on in. The coffee's hot."

4

THE SOUND OF HAMMERING AND SAWING filled the air. Gallows were going up, and the location was the site of the old Mossyhorn Saloon.

Joe said, "That's what my brother's old aunt would call irony."

"It is that," I said. "It's also the only spot available."

"I don't care if they hang him from a timber in the livery barn, as long as he's hanged."

I nodded. "I think we're all in agreement on that."

We could hear the men working on the gallows from inside my office. I've seen such a thing have a dampening effect on a man's spirits before, but if it was having any on Hooper, it wasn't evident. The man reclined on his bunk like he was having a vacation, reading a week-old newspaper that had come in on the stage.

I finally said to him, "Don't you realize what's going to happen tomorrow at noon?"

He said, not taking his eyes from the paper. "Shares of Del Penn Steel have gone up two dollars. Not bad."

I got to my feet and looked at him. "Just what kind of game are you playing?"

He looked over the top of the paper at me. "That man's no doctor, you know."

I hated the way he would do that. Play games with your mind, manipulating a conversation to work it against you. I decided not to play along and returned to my desk.

I was still procrastinating on that expense ledger. I had ridden with the Texas Rangers a short time and served as a deputy county sheriff once, but I never had to deal with the paperwork I did on this job. It seemed being town marshal was as much about expense verification and putting together an office budget as it was enforcing the law.

Hooper decided to carry on the conversation without me. He said, "That man is a gunfighter. You can tell by the way he walks."

"He set a broken arm this morning. Looked like a doctor to me."

Young Billy had been running across a street and not watching where he was going, and found himself under the hooves of a horse. Billy wound up breaking his arm just above the wrist. Not the large bone, but the smaller one that runs beside it. Doc Benson said it was the *ulna*, or some such thing. Sounded like Latin to me.

Benson had sat on a stool, reassuring Billy everything would be all right. With his jacket off and his shirtsleeves rolled up almost to his elbows, he had set the arm and applied a splint as well as I had ever seen it done. On a table across the room was his gunbelt and pistol. I tended not to miss this sort of thing, being something of a gunfighter myself.

Joe sat across from my desk, drinking coffee and saying nothing. But later in the afternoon, with Will standing guard over Hooper, I headed out to check the gallows and Joe came along with me.

As we walked along, Joe said, "When you think about it, what do we really know about that doctor? He don't move like no doctor I ever seen before. Something about the way he wears that gun, I think he knows how to use it."

"The man said he was in the War. A lot of men learned to fight really fast in that war. I was one of 'em."

"Still, I've never seen a doctor like him before."

"He has his degree hanging in a frame on the wall. Harvard Medical School. And he set Billy's arm like he's set a bone before."

I stopped walking and looked at Joe. "Don't let Hooper get to you. That's how a man like him controls people. Plants doubt in people's minds and then watches the seeds grow, and then finds a way to work it all against you."

Joe shook his head and gave a sort of grinning chuckle. "I should know better."

I slapped him in the shoulder. "Come on. Let's check those gallows. Then maybe we can go grab a whiskey."

We resumed walking.

Joe said, "Why do you suppose he's doing that? Trying to plant seeds of doubt in us? It's not like anything can come of it. He's gonna be swingin' by noon tomorrow."

"I've been giving that some thought myself. I'm thinking he's just not right in the head. After all, look at all the things he did. The things he was convicted of don't really cover all the crimes he committed. They were just the ones there was enough evidence to convict him on. Why would a man do all that?"

"Some folks just like to hurt others. Or to kill.

I've seen it before."

I nodded. "I think Hooper's like that. Something dark and twisted inside him. And tomorrow at noon, it becomes no longer our problem."

5

THE FOLLOWING MORNING, THE GALLOWS
were tested. A lever was pulled and the trapdoor fell
open. A grain sack filled with dirt was tied to a rope
overhead, and it dropped and then the fall was
stopped hard when the rope was pulled to full
extension.

I stood in front of my office with a cup of
coffee in hand. Joe was down by the gallows, as it
seemed like someone from our office should be there
supervising while the thing was being tested. But
even from this distance, I could hear the *thump* as the
grain bag gave its sudden pull against the rope.

Will was out walking the rounds. Doc Benson
stood beside me with a coffee cup in hand.

He said, "Are you expecting trouble this
morning?"

I said, "Whenever Jonathan Hooper is
involved, I expect trouble."

"Well, since I have to be on hand anyway, to
pronounce him dead, maybe I should be deputized.
Just in case. Might be good to have an extra man on
hand."

I looked at him. "All right. Consider yourself
deputized."

He grinned. "You don't stand much on
ceremony, do you?"

"Never have."

Once the coffee was finished, I gave Doc a
badge from my desk, and he headed back to his
office.

Hooper was inside his cell, stretched out on

the bunk in the cell. He was now just staring toward the ceiling. Even still, I found the company unpleasant and didn't want to deal with my ledger anymore, anyway, so I refilled my coffee cup and went back to the boardwalk outside my office.

I saw Jericho Long walking toward me. A tall, lanky kid in a shirt with sleeves that were a little too short for him, and a mop of hair that seemed to fly in various directions at once. He worked as a swamper at the saloon. I wasn't sure just when he had arrived in town or where he was from, but he had been here a few weeks.

He said, "Mornin', Marshal."

"Mornin', Jericho."

"I was just wonderin'," he looked down at his tattered work boots. "Well, what with the hangin' and all, I was wonderin' if you might need another man on hand."

Jericho, as a deputy? He looked like a broom was about all he could handle. But I didn't want to run him down, so I said, "Thanks, but I don't have the budget for any more deputies."

It was the truth. Doc Benson was working for free.

Jericho said, "You don't have to pay me, Marshal. It's just somethin' I always wanted. My grandfather was a Deputy U.S. Marshal. Worked his whole life as a lawman. I growed up on a farm in Ohio, but I always wanted to be a lawman. I come west to follow in his footsteps."

I looked at him. An awkward country boy who was all arms and legs. I said, "Do you even know how to fire a gun, Jericho?"

He nodded and gave a grin. A country boy, overloaded with exuberance. "Why, yes sir, Marshal. I'm a crack shot with a rifle."

I had a Winchester leaning against the wall. Considering I had Jonathan Hooper in my jail, I figured I should have a rifle on hand while I was standing outside.

"Take that rifle," I said. "Let's see if you can use it."

He grabbed the rifle and I stepped back a little. I half expected Jericho to shoot himself in the foot. Give Doc Benson a little business. But he jacked a cartridge into the chamber like he had done it before.

He said, "What you want me to shoot?"

Atop the livery barn, maybe five hundred feet away, was a weather vane. "Can you hit that weather vane on top of that roof?"

Not that I had anything against that weather vane, but I figured it was safe.

"Yes sir, Marshal."

Jericho brought the gun to his shoulder and sighted in, and fired. To my surprise, the weather vane began spinning around furiously as the bullet nicked it.

Jericho jacked another bullet in. "Now I'll make it spin the other way."

He brought the gun back to his shoulder and fired, and the vane began spinning the other way.

I was standing with my mouth hanging open. I had never seen a finer demonstration of shooting.

He said, "My grandfather showed me how to shoot. He knowed I wanted to be a lawman."

"What was his name?"

"Jedidiah Bell. He was my mother's father."

"Jed Bell." I nodded. "I've heard the name."

He smiled with country-boy pride. "Yes, sir. Most folks have, I reckon."

"But, why'd you come all the way out west like this, alone? Couldn't he give you some sort of letter of recommendation somewhere? He must have known people in law enforcement."

"Yes sir, he did. But I wanted to do this on my own. He became a lawman without no one pullin' strings for him. I wanted to do the same."

I gave him a long look. Sometimes there is just so much more to a person than you first thought that it startles you.

He held the rifle out for me to take.

"You hang onto it," I said. "Go inside my desk, top right drawer, and get yourself a badge."

6

I WAS sitting at my desk. Doc Benson was pacing the floor between my desk and the stove. The coffee pot was standing on the stove, now grown cold. Joe McCabe, the man called Smith, was sitting on one corner of my desk. Will Church was standing in the open doorway, leaning one shoulder against the door jamb. Jericho was sitting in an upright chair against one wall, polishing a Winchester.

I had seen this kind of thing before, in the final minutes before an execution. A kind of heaviness falls on everyone. Even though a man like Hooper in no way invited mercy, it wasn't lost on us that we would be escorting a man to die.

Doc pulled a pocket watch from his vest and flipped it open. "Eleven forty-five."

"It's time," I said, and pushed myself to my feet.

I turned toward the jail cell, reaching into my vest pocket for the key, and found Hooper on his feet just behind the bars, staring at us.

"I want you to know, Hooper," I said, "that I take no great pleasure in this. But the law has spoken."

"The law," he said, with a mixture of amusement and contempt. "And what is the law? Just the leaders of society deciding what is right and wrong. How is that any different from what I was doing in this town before you came along?"

"It's different."

"I pronounced judgment on people. Sentenced some of them to die. How is that different from what you are doing now?"

I shook my head. "This is not the time for a debate."

I pushed the key into the lock and turned it. The door opened. Doc Benson was there with a gun ready, as was Joe. Will had stepped fully into the room and Jericho had gotten to his feet and had a loaded Winchester in his hands.

Sam Wilson poked his head in the doorway. "You boys want an extra hand? There's an angry mob out here, and a long walk to the gallows."

I said, "Thanks, Sam. I'd welcome all the help we can get."

Hooper held his wrists out in front of him and I locked the cuffs on.

"Beware the avenging angel," Hooper said.

I looked at him wearily. I was in no mood for his games.

"Come on," I said.

"How do you want to do this?" Doc said.

"Joe can step out first. Keep that scattergun ready. Nothing like a scattergun to get people's attention."

Joe nodded.

I wasn't really betraying anything by calling him Joe in public. I had done so a few times and people had started referring to him as Joe Smith.

I said, "I'll follow immediately with the prisoner. Then I want Jericho right behind me, and Will to one side and you, Doc, to the other."

Hooper was grinning. "Do you really plan to shoot any of the good citizens of your town if they try to put a bullet in me? To rob you all of the spectacle of seeing me swing from a noose?"

"I'm hoping we don't have to. I'm hoping the fire power we have here will make anyone think twice."

We started out. Joe first. Then Hooper and me. I was the only one without a shoulder arm. I walked beside Hooper, on his right, so he would not be within reach of the gun holstered at my own right side. Then came Jericho immediately behind us, gripping the Winchester with both hands. He was no longer a boy but not quite a man. Fresh from the farm and looking out of place, and yet he carried that Winchester like he was born to it. I knew by the look in his eye he was up to the job. To my right was Will, and Doc was over to Hooper's left.

I walked with my left hand gripping Hooper's arm. He shook me loose and said, "I can walk on my own."

There was a crowd in front of us, maybe a couple hundred people. Not only residents from here in town, but folks from the outlying ranches. They parted to form a natural aisle for us to pass through.

We came to the gallows. The noose was hanging empty, waiting for Hooper. At the top of the steps was Tyler Garrett, the leader of the town council. He had been the one chosen to pull the lever. The pastor of the Baptist church was standing beside him. He wore a dark gray suit and a string tie, and in his hands was a Bible.

Joe began climbing the stairs, with Hooper and me right behind him. Doc Benson came up with us, also. He was now in his double role as attending physician as well as deputy.

The minister began, "Are there any words you would like spoken? Would you like to ask your Lord Jesus into your heart?"

Hooper said, "Get away from me."

I motioned Hooper over toward the trap door. He strolled across the platform as though he was just casually walking about, and stopped on the door.

He said, "I do not see Miss Shannon in the crowd."

I still hadn't told him that Maddie left town shortly after he was arrested and no one had heard from her since. I didn't think he had the right to know just what kind of pain he had caused her.

I said, "It's likely you won't."

"So, my last request, a chance to speak with her, will be denied."

"I think there's good money on that."

I stepped aside and Garrett approached with a black hood in one hand.

"No," Hooper said. "As my last request, since I am to be denied Miss Shannon's company, is to be free of that hood. If you are all to snuff out a man's life, I want you to have to look into his eyes as you do so."

Garrett looked at me. He was the authority here, but he clearly didn't know what to do.

I said, "It's not an easy thing we do here, today. No killing should ever be. When you look into the eyes of the man you have to kill, it stays with you. And that's the way it should be."

"Amen," the minister said.

Doc looked at me. He had been in the war. He had killed. He knew what I was talking about—I could see it in his eyes.

Garrett reached for the noose, then hesitated a moment, like he thought Hooper was a wild animal and might bite him. But then he pulled the noose down over Hooper's head and tightened it around his neck. He then went to the wooden lever. To pull it would release the trap door.

"Any last words?" he said.

Hooper looked down at the crowd before him. "Beware the avenging angel. All of you."

Garrett looked to me. I gave a nod of my head. He pulled the lever and the trap door opened and Hooper fell through. The rope pulled tight with a loud *thump*, and Hooper's body jerked sharply, and he was dead. His neck, broken. His feet twitched and shook a few moments, then he was still.

One woman screamed. A man let out a loud, cheering hoot. But most of the crowd just stood in silence. Then they began to disperse.

Doc Benson pronounced Hooper dead, and the body was carted off to the undertaker. Joe and I headed for the saloon. I never liked executions. They might be necessary, they might not. Such things are for philosophers and politicians to debate. But it always left me with a bad feeling.

I said to the bartender, "Give me a bottle."

He knew I drank bourbon generally, so he gave me a bottle of his best, and Joe and I went to a table. Jericho and Will followed us in.

I said to Jericho, "How old are you?"

"Nineteen. Not old enough to drink."

"You are today. Sit down."

Doc Benson came into the saloon and grabbed a glass from the bartender and joined us at the table.

He said, "What do you suppose that meant? That thing he said. His last words. He said the same thing in the jail."

"Beware the avenging angel," Will said.

I shook my head. "More of his cryptic nonsense. Trying to play with our minds, up to the very end."

Joe said, "Well, it's done. He's gone. We don't have to worry about him no more."

Sam Wilson stepped into the saloon. He stood in the doorway a moment, looking around the room. He found us and came on over.

"Got a little news I wanted to share," he said. "I waited until after the hanging. I figured you had enough on your mind and needed to focus on the task at hand."

"I hope it's good news," I said, staring at the glass of whiskey in my hand.

Sam nodded, smiling. "Got me a letter. It arrived just yesterday. From Saint Louis. From Maddie."

That got my attention.

Sam said, "She's coming back. Maddie's coming home."

PART TWO
THE RETURN

7

I TRIED to sit calmly. I tried to look nonchalant. But my heart wanted to jump out of my chest.

I stared into the glass of whiskey in my hand and said nothing, but there was no fooling Joe. He knew me too well. I could see him out of the corner of my eye. Joe wasn't one to smile openly or say a lot, but he glanced at me and beneath his huge, juniper bush of a beard, he grinned.

He saved me from having to ask the obvious question. That's what good friends do. He said, "So, when's she due in?"

Sam was smiling like a cheshire cat. Nothing was lost on him, either.

He said, "You know how mail is. Takes forever to get a letter from back east to here. Even from Saint Louie. She sent this over a month ago. But she gave the date. She should be arriving on the stage next Thursday."

Doc Benson said, "So, who is this Maddie woman?"

"An old friend," Joe said.

Sam nodded and smiled. "She's like a daughter to me. It'll be good to have her back where she belongs. The ranch has been empty without her."

This gave me a lot to think about.

The talk grew more light-hearted after that. Sam grabbed a seat and a glass. Eventually, the barkeep brought over another bottle. Jericho showed that though he was under the drinking age, he drank his whiskey like a professional. He knocked back one glassful, then poured another. I was realizing there was a lot more to this young man than I had first thought.

We all chatted and laughed. Doc Benson had been an officer in the late War Betwixt the States. He told stories of battles.

He told one story where they had brought in a soldier dead from the battlefield. A bullet hole was in his chest, and blood smeared all over the front of his uniform. He was Catholic so a chaplain said last rites over him, and then a buddy of his opened a bottle of whiskey. He wanted to have one last drink in his buddy's honor.

Doc Benson said, "So this soldier, he held up the glass and said, 'My old friend, this last glass of whiskey is for you.' Then the dead soldier done sat up and grabbed the glass of whiskey right out of his friend's hand and said, 'Don't mind if I do,' and slugged it back.

"Turned out, he wasn't shot. The hole in his uniform was from an accident with his own bayonet a couple of months earlier. The blood on his uniform was from another soldier who had been shot and landed on top of him. Knocked him down and he hit his head on a rock, and was knocked clear out."

We all laughed like idiots. Not that the story was all that funny, but when you've had a little too much whiskey, things seem a whole lot funnier.

Doc said, "The chaplain giving the last rights, he done turned white as a sheet and fell right over."

Doc Benson normally had an eloquent way of

speaking. Not unlike a Shakespearean actor. But when he got some whiskey in him, a bit of a Kentucky twang seemed to come out.

I had noticed long ago that if you get men sitting around a table or a campfire and get some whiskey into them, they'll tell you things about themselves that they never intended to tell. Such as that Doc Benson might have an educated way about him and speak like a thespian, but he was actually from the hills of Kentucky.

At one point, I said, "Doc, I hope you don't mind this bourbon."

I said this because most men I had met preferred straight-up whiskey. Bourbon is more of a southern thing. Even though I was from Missouri, I had developed a taste for it over the years.

Doc said, "Not at all. It's been too long since I've tasted good old fashioned Kentucky bourbon."

And so we all talked and laughed. Jericho told stories about some fancy shooting he had done. He said someone once tossed a silver dollar in the air and he shot the center out of it, and then when it was on its way down, he jacked the rifle quickly and shot the second bullet also through the center. The men all laughed, and Doc slapped him on the back and refilled his glass. Thing was, I had seen Jericho shoot and I don't think he was exaggerating.

After a time, I sort of sat back in the chair and let the talking and laughing continue while I thought about Maddie.

I would never profess to know a thing about love. But I know there wasn't a day went by that I didn't think about that girl. And now she was coming back. She was coming here.

I had to wonder. Was she coming back to me?

The previous summer had been a complicated time, emotionally. She had been in love with me—of that, I was sure. But she also had a powerful hate for Jonathan Hooper. The man had killed her father, at least as far as we knew. There was never any proof that he had paid to have Nathan Shannon killed, and I had learned never to take much stock in something that couldn't be proven. But Maddie fully believed Hooper was behind the murder, and had been within a whisker of killing the man, and then realized that if she did, it would have brought her down to his level.

In a way, Jonathan Hooper sort of came between Maddie and me. Maddie and her father and Sam Wilson had built their ranch back in the old days of Texas, when the only law was the law that you carried in your holster. They had defended their ranch against rustlers and Mexican border raiders and Comanche renegades. Maddie, as a girl of seventeen, had stood with a rifle against her shoulder alongside her father and Sam, defending their ranch.

And when Jonathan Hooper drifted in and began taking over the nearby town of Wardtown and building a small criminal empire, her reaction was to fight back not by seeking out law-enforcement officers, but by grabbing a Winchester. Then I came in, representing the law, and we found ourselves at odds. She wanted to put a bullet in Hooper, and I wanted to arrest him so he could stand trial.

The thing was, since we were in love, we now had a conflict that gave Maddie even more emotional distress. Once I arrested Hooper, Maddie headed back east to stay with her mother a while.

I never really knew the whole story of Maddie's parents. I knew Sam Wilson did, but I never thought it was my place to ask. If Maddie had wanted me to know, she would have told me. But from what I gathered, her mother and father were married and lived for a while at the ranch, back in the early days. But her mother could never quite adapt to living on a ranch out in the wilds of Texas. She had come from a privileged life in St. Louis, and eventually returned to it and took the young Maddie with her. Maddie grew up in St. Louis, but spent her summers on the ranch with her father and Sam, and once she was eighteen, went to live with them.

When Maddie left to go stay with her mother, she was vague about how long she would be gone. I had the impression she might be back some day, or not at all. Maybe she did this intentionally because she didn't want me to feel I had to wait for her. Or maybe she didn't truly know herself if she would ever be back.

There was a young widow by the name of Nell who had moved to town and was running a restaurant, and she smiled at me a couple of times and I could have invited her into my life. At one point I thought I was foolish not to, since it was possible Maddie might never return. And even if she did, the love might not still be there. She and I had never made commitments to each other. And yet, I couldn't get her out of my thoughts. It wouldn't have been fair to Nell, so I never gave her the invitation.

And now Maddie was coming back. All these months later. It felt like it had been years.

Everyone was laughing, and they looked at me. Three other men had joined us. Cowhands who worked for Sam. Really, they worked for Maddie, but Sam was running the ranch in her absence. They all looked to me because I wasn't laughing, but I had been too lost in thought to even hear what they had been talking about.

Sam was grinning wide and said, "I know what he's been thinking about."

And they all laughed again. Men were slapping me on the back. I took another drink of bourbon, and I went back to thinking about Maddie.

8

AFTER A TIME, JOE AND DOC BENSON decided to start chasing their whiskey with beer. They would toss back a glassful and then follow it with a mouthful of beer. I knew this was a mistake, and I knew what would be awaiting these two come morning.

I knew me an old scout years ago. He had told me the best way to avoid a hangover was to drink straight whiskey. Not to mix it with anything, and to make sure and drink water while you're doing it. Try to get one good chug of water for every glass of whiskey

I was just a young buck when I rode with him, and I told him I didn't like straight-up whiskey. It burned on the way down and I told him I didn't like that. He told me the proper way to drink whiskey was to first hold your breath and then take an ounce of it on the tongue, then swallow it, and then slowly let your breath out. I found he was right. If you do this with whiskey, there's a smoky, woody flavor that sort of drifts up through you. If you do it with bourbon, then the taste is much more subtle but it has the same effect.

I found he was right about how to drink whiskey, and he was right about hangovers, too.

The following morning, Joe and Doc were paying for their lack of knowledge. We were at Nell's restaurant. Joe was rubbing his eyes and holding his head, and drinking coffee like it was medicine from heaven. Doc was in a white shirt and jacket but hadn't even attempted a tie this morning, and he had said his head hurt so bad it was painful to even put on his hat.

Me, I was just sipping coffee. I had slept like a baby the night before and felt great.

Nell came over. She was maybe in her late twenties and as prctty as you can get. Easily as pretty as Maddie. She had dark hair but eyes that were an almost eerie shade of light gray. She had a smile that could light up a room. If it hadn't been for Maddie I surely would have been returning her smiles right from the start.

She offered more coffee, and Joe and Doc nodded their heads but said nothing, as though the very act of speaking caused pain.

She gave me a smile. A broad, inviting grin. I nodded and gave a polite smile.

I was probably out of my mind, I thought. Maddie and I had never professed our love for each other. We had never talked about commitment or about building a life together. I just didn't think it would be fair to Nell to return the smile and start getting to know her when Maddie was still on my mind.

Doc Benson said to me, "How do you do it? You drank as much whiskey as we did last night, but you're sitting there like all is well with the world. How do you do it?"

I didn't want to tell him my secret. I found this all too amusing. I said, "Old Apache medicine trick."

Benson gave me a look that said he didn't believe that for a second, but his head hurt too much to pursue it.

Joe said, "So, what're you going to do?"
I said, "About what?"

"About what Hooper said?"

It occurred to me that I had apparently drank more whiskey the night before than I realized. I said, "What did he say?"

"The bit about the avenging angel."

Oh, that.

I said, "Hooper had a way of getting into people's minds. I think that might have been the real power he had over people. But he's dead. We're going to bury him today, outside of town. Boot hill. He's gone and he's not coming back. I think it's time that we just let him be gone, and got on with our lives."

Doc Benson nodded. Made sense to him. Joe nodded, too.

Nell came back over. She glanced at Benson and Joe and said, "Is there a sickness going around that I should know about?"

I grinned. "Nothing that a couple more pots of coffee won't cure."

She gave me an understanding nod, and said, "More coffee, coming right up."

I said, "They will be ever so grateful."

Doc gave me a look with bleary eyes and said, "You're finding this outright amusing."

I said, "I have to admit, I am."

9

BILLY HAD a splint on one arm, but he could still ride a horse. I sent him out to the Shannon ranch with the message that I needed a couple hands who knew how to use a shovel. Sam sent two men in, and I took them out to a place just beyond the last building in town. There were a few graves here. Cowhands or drifters who had gotten themselves shot, and there was no family to claim the body. We didn't even know the name of one man. His wooden grave marker just read UNKNOWN. SHOT JANUARY 1875. We found a suitable spot and the two cowhands commenced to digging.

We called the place Boot Hill, even though it wasn't really a hill. The term had started in Dodge City, up Kansas way. I never heard the actual reason for the term, but it was for men who died and didn't belong to anyone. The term had caught on, and now pretty much any type of pauper's cemetery in the west was called by that name.

I stood with a cup of Nell's coffee in my hand while the two dug, then I spelled one of them, taking off my vest and rolling up my sleeves.

The whole town and then some had turned out to watch Jonathan Hooper be hanged. He had taken over the town by forcing out the business owners, and then appointed himself judge and jury. He had ordered men hanged. He had tried to force Maddie Shannon into joining him on a crusade of lawless intimidation with the eventual goal of attaining a seat in the United States Senate. But in the end, when his corpse was wrapped in a sheet of canvas and dropped into the Texas earth, only three people turned out. Myself, Doc Benson and Joe.

The two hands Sam had sent out lowered the body down into the grave. It landed hard with a *thump.*

"Strangely non-poetic," Doc Benson said.

He was no longer drunk, and the Tennessee twang was gone from his voice like it had never been there.

"It is that," I said.

Even the town minister hadn't bothered to turn out. A man about forty who had moved to town a few weeks ago. Ebenezer Crumby, he had told me his name was. A Baptist minister. He didn't wear a white collar, because Baptist ministers usually don't. He conducted his services in a tie and jacket. I wasn't much for church, but he strolled down to Nell's every so often for morning coffee, and I had gotten to know him there. He had told me to call him Eb. But here was a man's earthly remains being dropped into the ground, and even Eb hadn't turned out to say a prayer or to say, "Ashes to ashes." Seemed to me a minister should at least be present to say that.

Doc Benson also had a cup of Nell's coffee in one hand as he stood there, beside me. He was no longer bleary-eyed, but still hadn't managed to put on his tie.

He looked at me and said, "Any final words?"

I appreciated poetry and a good sermon, and though I wasn't a church-going man, I believed in the words from the Good Book. Especially Paul's writings from Romans and Galations. But I had no illusions about being a well-spoken man. I would leave the sermons and the poetry to those better suited to it than I.

I said, "God help him."

Joe said, "Amen."

Doc looked at the two cowhands with the shovels and said, "Cover him over."

And that was that. A strangely quiet, subdued end to one of the most notorious me who had ever set foot on Texas soil.

We went back to Nell's—Doc Benson, Joe and me. I had left Jericho in charge of the office. Should any great crime wave break out, he would be there.

We sat down and Nell refilled our cups. She smiled at me and I gave a polite grin and a nod of my head. Then she gave the exact same smile to Doc. Maybe she was getting tired of waiting for me. Doc wasn't too hung-over to notice. He looked a little surprised at first, and then returned the smile.

He let his eyes follow her as she walked away. Without being too inappropriate, a young woman has a way of walking that can catch a man's eye. Some women try to enhance it with a little extra sway of the hips, but others just have a subtle and yet entrancing way of moving. Nell was one of that second group. Doc sat and watched her walk back to the kitchen. Even though my thoughts were of Maddie, I was still a man and I couldn't help but notice, either. And even Joe, who was one of the most emotionally subdued men I had ever met, watched her walk away with a grin beneath his beard.

Then Doc took a sip of his coffee and looked

at me and said, "So, tell me about this Maddie Shannon woman."

And so I did.

Doc Benson was about as different from me as a man could get, at least on the surface. He was a doctor, an educated man. A man of sophistication, where I couldn't even tie a tie properly. And yet, I knew he could use that gun he strapped to his leg. The knuckles of both hands bore the scars of a man who had been in his share of fist-fights. When he rode a horse, he didn't just sit on the saddle and bounce along like a lot of men did. He rode the horse like he and the horse were one.

Old horsemen had a saying. They said a man sat *in* the horse. That old scout who had taught me how to drink whiskey had said it about me. Sam Wilson and Joe McCabe both did this. And so did Doc Benson.

Even though I had no idea how this man of education was every bit as much a gunfighter as I was, there was a sort of camaraderie forming between us. And so, when he asked about Maddie, I told him. I wasn't usually one to talk much about myself, but I told him how I had ridden into town, sent by Captain McNelly of the Texas Rangers. I had been sent to observe Jonathan Hooper, and if I thought anything was amiss, to arrest him. I told Doc of how Maddie and I had fallen in love, but her desire for old-fashioned frontier justice had been in conflict with my duties as a law officer, and in the end, that conflict had pulled us apart.

Benson said, "There's something Shakespearean about all of that."

I knew nothing of Shakespeare.

I said, "Maybe so. But here I am, waiting for her like a damned fool. For all I know, she's put me long behind her."

"Then why would she be coming back here?"

"Because of her ranch. Her father and Sam Wilson built that place out of the Texas grasslands. They built that place from absolutely nothing. And now, it belongs to Maddie and Sam. Too much of her life's blood runs through it for her to be away from it for too long."

Doc glanced at Joe. "Do you think that's it? Do you think that's why she's coming back?"

Joe shrugged. "I've had better luck predicting the shuffle of a deck of cards than I have a woman's heart."

Doc took a sip of coffee. "Maybe it's just that I've read too much romantic poetry. I took a class in it once back at school. But there's a potentially great love story building here."

My turn to shrug. I said, "I just don't want to get my hopes up."

Joe took a sip of his coffee. Nell's coffee was the kind that made you stop and savor the taste. Then he paused thoughtfully for a moment and said, "I have a brother. He met this girl and they fell in love. The look they had in their eyes when they looked at each other was like nothing I had ever seen before. Until I saw you and Maddie."

He was looking at me.

Doc grinned at me. "She's coming back for you, old hoss."

10

I HOPED they were right. I hoped Maddie was coming back for me. And yet, I refused to allow myself to have hope.

Maybe there had been too many disappointments in my life. After the War, I had returned home, hoping to resume the life that had once been mine. The life of a Missouri farm boy. But I found our farm house burned to the ground. The place had been attacked by guerilla raiders during the war. The graves of Ma and Pa were out behind the empty foundation of our home.

They had received word by mistake months earlier that I had died in battle. They had gone to the great beyond believing I was dead. My brother Morgan, feeling there was nothing left for him in Missouri, had ridden west. He had been gone a few months when I returned.

I rode west looking for him. There were times when I arrived in a town or a cow camp just weeks behind him. But eventually, I lost all trace of him. It was like he had fallen off the proverbial face of the Earth. I never found him.

As such, I learned not to put much stock in the thing called *hope*.

I had wandered here and there. I took jobs doing such things as riding shotgun for a stage line. At one time, I learned my former commanding officer had retired to New Mexico territory. When I rode in for a visit, I found Mexican border raiders had attacked and kidnapped his daughter, and so I rode into Mexico to rescue her. Another time, I took a job scouting for the Army in their war against the Apache.

Eventually, my journeys led me to Texas. Leander McNelly, captain of the Texas Rangers, needed a man to ride into Wardtown undercover. He needed a capable man but who wouldn't be known. I was referred to him because most of my exploits had been outside of Texas. Once I had arrested Jonathan Hooper, I decided to end my wanderings and make this little town my home.

I tried to convince myself that Maddie's homecoming would be inconsequential to me. Nothing for me to get all stirred up over. After all, I didn't need more disappointment in my life.

Every morning I met Doc Benson for coffee at Nell's. Joe actually worked for Sam, but sometimes he would ride in to join us. Sometimes Sam would come with him. Occasionally Jericho or Will would join us, or Pastor Eb from the church.

One day led to another, and finally the day was upon us. Thursday. The day the stage came through town.

I had a bath and shave that morning. For no reason in particular, I told myself.

Joe was in town that morning. Sam rode with him. They joined Doc and me for coffee at Nell's.

When she filled Doc's cup, she gave him a broad smile and had an extra light in her eye. He returned the smile. When she looked at me, it was just a polite smile and nothing more. Apparently Doc had replaced me in Nell's eyes, but I wasn't disappointed at all in this. Nell was a good woman, and Doc was a good man.

Jericho was there, too. And Will Church.

I said to Jericho, "Who's minding the store?"

"Oh, if any trouble happens, they'll know where to find us."

Everyone was here for the same reason. They wanted to see what would happen when Maddie got off that stage.

I shook my head at the thought. I hoped they wouldn't be too disappointed. After all, Maddie had been gone for more than six months, and there hadn't been one letter. I had a hard time believing that I was foremost in her thoughts. Sam had arrived with a buggy, and I was sure Maddie would be climbing into it and he would be driving her out to the ranch, and that would be all there was to it.

"Oh," Sam said. "I forgot to mention this. Her mother's coming with her. Amelia. She was off in Europe when Nathan died. I suppose she's come to pay her respects."

"Well, that's good," I said. "Her mother coming out here to do that, and to be with her."

Sam looked at me pitifully. "You've never met Amelia McAllister Shannon."

There was silence at the table. I said, "No, I haven't."

Sam said no more about it, but he didn't look happy. He focused on his cup of coffee. I looked at Joe, and he shrugged.

The morning wore on. I went back to the office. There was paperwork I never seemed to get to. Reward posters that needed to be nailed to the wall. I never took this part of the job seriously, because I had never known anyone to look at a reward poster and say, "Well, I know that feller, and I know where he is." Reward posters never helped the law catch a felon. It was just more work for a town marshal to do.

Joe sat on the edge of the desk. Sam paced back and forth nervously.

"What has gotten you so worked up?" Joe finally said.

"Just the thought of Amelia being here. I'd love to see Maddie again. But her mother causes problems wherever she goes. The woman could start a range war if she stays long enough. I've never met anyone who acts so innocent and yet is actively looking for trouble. Had she been living here over the years, Jonathan Hooper wouldn't have stood a chance."

Jericho still had his job as a saloon swamper, but he meandered over to the office. Will was leaning against a wall, finishing off a hand-rolled smoke. Doc Benson was there, too.

I said, "Don't you have any patients to attend to?"

He said, "If there are any, they'll know where to find me."

I said, "I can't believe you're all here to see her get off the stage."

Jericho said, "There's a whole crowd forming, down there at the stage depot."

I looked at him in disbelief. "Most of the folks here in town weren't even here back when Maddie was. They don't even know her."

Doc shrugged. "I suppose they've all heard about the great love between you two."

I was starting to grow a little exasperated.

"There's no guarantee she's come back for me. She never even sent one letter the whole time she was gone."

"I guess everyone is just hoping."

I looked at Doc like he had spoken Greek, so he said, "Everyone likes a good love story, Tremain. Most people go through their whole lives hoping for the kind of love we all hear you and Miss Shannon had. If it can happen to someone they know, then there's still hope for them. It's about hope."

I suppose I couldn't argue with that. But at the same time, I wasn't going to let myself indulge in the hope that she was coming back to me.

Finally, we heard the sounds of the stage rolling down the street. Dime novels make it out that a stage goes everywhere with its horses at a full gallop, but that just ain't so. Drivers tended to pace their teams, often keeping them at little more than a spirited walk. That was how the stage came into town. We heard the horses, and the jingle and creak of the stage itself.

"Here she is," Sam said, and hurried out through the door.

I was still sitting behind my desk.

Joe looked at me impatiently. "Well?"

I gave a weary sigh. "All right. Let's get this over with."

I rose from the desk. My gunbelt was in the drawer, and I didn't bother to reach for it. It was Thursday. Around here, nowadays, the only time I needed my gun was on Saturday night.

I headed out the door and down toward the stage depot. Doc Benson was behind me, and behind him were Joe and Will and Jericho. I felt like the Pied Piper.

I saw old Hank climbing down from the stage. A Mexican man was sitting up there, too. Maybe fifty, with a dusty, flat-brimmed sombrero. One of the first things I noticed about a man was how he wore his gun, and this man wore his high on his hip. This meant he was probably not a fast draw and wasn't trying to be. Didn't mean he didn't know how to shoot, though.

Hank pulled open the door, and a woman stepped out. She was as tall as I was, with dark hair and a hat pinned to it. She stood regally.

She called up to the top of the stage, "Julio, get my trunks."

I said howdy to Hank, and said, "New man?"

The woman said, "Hardly, Marshal. He works for me. It wouldn't do for the hired help to ride in the coach with his employer."

She stood ramrod straight, and her eyes reminded me of a mountain lion surveying a herd of sheep and deciding which one to devour first. I had seen eyes like this on hardened killers. Most recently, the man we had put in Boot Hill a week ago.

Then her eyes then landed on Sam, and I thought I saw them soften a bit.

"Sam," she said.

"Amelia."

"It's good to see you."

He said, "Wish I could say the same."

I glanced at him. Such conduct toward a woman was just not done in those days, especially in public. Even here on the frontier, a man was expected to have courtesy toward a woman.

But I saw the look in his eye. It was more than anger. I saw hurt there.

Sam said, "Everyone, I would like you to meet Amelia McAllister Shannon."

She nodded to the crowd about her, as though she were some sort of royalty or debutante.

Then I heard a woman's voice from inside the stage, behind her. A voice I knew all too well. A voice that made my heart pound a little harder.

"Mother, are you going to stand there all day?"

Amelia gave a little sigh, as though she were greatly annoyed but trying not to show it, but in doing so showed it all too well. Then she stepped down from the stage. Hank offered her a hand as she did so, but she ignored it.

Then Maddie stepped out. She was in a green dress that reached all the way to the ground. A ruffled neckline. A little low cut, enough to catch the eye but not enough to look overbearing. Her hair was done up like some woman from a New York catalogue, and she had a hat made of green velvet and lace pinned to it.

She looked at me. Our eyes met. I felt something bitingly cold and yet extremely hot wash over me.

Amelia McAllister Shannon saw the way Maddie and I looked at each other. She said, "Oh, you're *that* marshal."

Hank offered his hand to Maddie, but she was too busy bolting from the stage to take it, landing on the ground in one leap despite her dress. Then she then began running toward me.

Amelia said, "Madelyn! Oh, for goodness sake, there goes your hat."

Maddie's hat had fallen away. I guess New York-style hats that were pinned to a lady's hair weren't meant for jumping and running.

Maddie had grabbed her dress with both hands to lift the hem a couple of inches so she wouldn't trip over it.

She then leaped at me and her arms were around me and mine were around her, and we were kissing like this was just what we were born to do. I lifted her off the ground and spun her around. Somewhere in all of this my hat went tumbling away. A cup of coffee had been in one hand, but now it was gone like it had never been there. Maddie's hair somehow came loose and fell down along her back.

Her mother said, "Madelyn. For goodness sake. You're embarrassing yourself."

I heard Sam say, "Amelia, do us all a favor and shut up."

I hadn't realized people had come out of the general store and the seamstress's shop and the cobbler's place and the hotel and had lined the street. But then they started to clap their hands and hoot and holler.

I spun Maddie around and we kissed like there was no tomorrow. Then we just stood there and her head was on my shoulder and her arms were wrapped around me. Her tears were soaking into my shirt and my own face was wet.

"I missed you so much," she said.

I found myself saying, "Not a day went by

that I wasn't thinking about you."

And Joe and Sam were slapping my back and Doc yelled, "Hip hip, hooray!" And people were cheering.

Then I said the words I had never actually said to her. Not really. I said, "I love you, Mad. I love you so much."

She nodded. Then she looked up at me with those incredible green eyes. The first time I had seen her, I thought a man could drown in those eyes. And I had, more than once.

She had long rivulets of tears running down her face, and she said, "I love you too. You know that."

I hadn't known that. Not really. She had been gone over six months with no word to me at all. And yet, as I looked in those eyes, I found myself saying, "I know that. I always have."

And then I pulled her in, not for a kiss, but for a long hug. Her arms were wrapped around me, too. It was like we couldn't pull each other in close enough. It was like we never wanted to let go.

The folks around us began to applaud again. First one person clapped, then another, then it was like we were at a theater house. And people were cheering. One man, it might have been Jericho or Sam, let out a high-pitched, "Yeeee-haw!" And a gun went off, and then another. And then a couple of cowhands were riding up and down the street shooting and cheering.

But Maddie and paid it all no mind, because despite the crowd swarming around us and all of the ruckus, there was just the two of us.

11

AMELIA McCALLISTER SHANNON WAS
extremely peeved at us. I found out two days later
when Sam said to me, "Amelia is really peeved at the
two of you."

You see, when two people love each other like
Maddie and I do, things like manners seem to fall
away without us even being aware of it at first. It can
be little things, like that fine hat Maddie had been
wearing when she first stepped off the stage. It had
come unpinned and fell away when she ran toward
me. Her mother had paid good money for it in St.
Louis, more than I made in three months as the
marshal of Wardtown. But Maddie had never
retrieved it. It got trampled underfoot by the crowd
that had turned out to see Maddie and me reunited,
and then got trampled even more by the cowhands
who were galloping up and down the street firing
their guns off. There had apparently been a feather
attached to it at one point.

I found out later that Jericho had discovered it
the next day by a water trough, hopelessly driven out
of shape and with dust and dirt pounded into it. He set
it up out behind the livery and used it for target
practice.

Another thing was Maddie's hair coming
loose. It might seem like a small thing, but a grown
woman in 1877 didn't go around with her hair

hanging loose. The only ones who did that were little girls and saloon women. Maddie's mother had worked hard to fix her hair all up in some sort of fancy New York do, and had used four hair pins to hold it in place. Maddie had very thick hair that fell almost to her waist, and I have to admit at the risk of not seeming like a gentleman, I loved to run my hands through it, and I thought she was at her most beautiful when her hair was hanging free. Her hair had come loose as soon as she leaped off the stage, and her hair pins were never found.

Then there was a more telling thing. The fact that Maddie abandoned her mother for two days.

Sam Wilson managed to somehow bring in two buggies from the ranch that morning without me being aware he had done it. Apparently, I had been so focused on Maddie's return and trying not to be too hopeful that I had missed it. One of the buggies was of the single-seat variety. This was what he was going to use to drive Amelia out to the ranch. There was also a two-seater, and a ranch hand was waiting with it. The hand was a young man I knew as Clem. Tall and with wild-looking hair, and a strong Virginia sound to his speech.

Sam said, "Marshal, Miss Shannon, this buggy is for the both of you."

I said, "The both of us?"

"Yes, sir. Climb on in."

So we did.

Clem then clicked the horse along. Maddie leaned into me and my arm was wrapped around her. Any thought of decorum had been thrown to the wind. She didn't even have her luggage.

After a while, Clem turned off the trail.

"Clem," I said. "Where are you taking us?"

"Ain't supposed to tell you," he said. "It's a surprise."

He said the word as *surprahse*. That Virginia accent of his.

Turned out Sam had outfitted one of the ranch's line shacks for Maddie and me. He hadn't told me about it at all. These line shacks were positioned at the outer edges of the ranch, and normally he had two or three hands stationed at each one. Most ranches had set-ups like this, and some of them referred to the cowhands stationed at the line shacks as the floating outfit, or the floaters. Clem told me Sam had recalled the men from this shack back to the ranch's headquarters.

We approached the shack, and Clem gave the reins a tug and brought the team to a full halt.

He said, "Sam told me this place is for the both of you, for as long as you want it."

"I truly appreciate Sam doing this," I said. "But it doesn't go far in the direction of discretion. I don't want anyone to think bad of Maddie."

Clem smiled. "Ain't no one gonna think bad of you two. You got the kind of love you only read about in fairy tales."

He climbed down from the wagon seat, and said, "'Sides everyone knows you're gonna get married sooner or later."

I looked at Maddie. She gave a shrug of her shoulders.

A horse was saddled and waiting for Clem. He stepped up and into the saddle, tipped his hat to us, and rode away.

Maddie and I were still in the back seat. My arm was around her, pulling her as tightly into me as could be.

The line shack was nothing more than a sod hut, and was surrounded by long, low hills that were covered with grass. In the corral were a couple of horses standing idly by, and there were the two horses still hitched to the buggy. Other than that, Maddie and I were totally alone.

I said, "Now, what can we possibly find to do with ourselves, way out here in the middle of nowhere?"

She didn't even bother to use words. Her mouth found mine, and the long kiss that had begun in town was resumed.

I went to start down from the wagon, but she was still attached to me and we fell to the grass. One of the horses looked at us and rolled its eyes, as if to say, *Oh, really*.

Maddie and I laughed. We laughed hard. Then she jumped onto me and we were lying in the grass, and we were kissing and touching. We didn't even make it into the line shack.

12

IT WAS DARK, AND Texas nights have a way of turning off cooler than you might think. Sam had anticipated this, and the wood box was over-flowing with firewood.

When Maddie had gone to St. Louis, she had left some clothes behind in her closet. Sam had taken it upon himself to go into that closet and bring some things out here to the line shack. A couple of changes of clothes and some night gowns.

I had brought nothing with me, but Sam had thought of that and made sure I had some shirts out here and an extra pair of jeans and some socks. How he had gotten these things out of my office without me knowing it left me amazed. I must have been much more distracted than I had realized. I had left my gunbelt back in town, but Sam had even thought of that, making sure there were three rifles and a box of ammunition.

Maddie was in a nightgown now, lying on one of the bunks. I was starting a fire in the small iron stove.

She said, "Mother is going to think I'm shameless. Well, I suppose she already does."

I looked back at her with a grin. "Shameless is a word for it."

She gave me a grin. "I don't hear you complaining."

The fire was going, so I shut the door to the stove. A bottle of wine was standing on the stable. Sam had thought of this, too. It was something called Pinot Noir. I had called it like it was spelled, but

Maddie laughed and said it was pronounced *pinyo nwar*. My name was French, so I was told, but I knew nothing of the language.

Sam had provided a cork screw. I put it to work and the cork came out with a *pop,* and we laughed like people always do when a cork does that. I filled two goblets and brought them to the bed.

Maddie and I had done little talking in the hours we had been here. We had just hugged and cuddled during the long ride out here. And then, at the risk of seeming less than a gentleman, we had been busy reuniting.

Now she said, "You know, I meant every word I said in my letters."

Letters? I looked at her with surprise as sat on the bed beside her.

She said, "My letters. The ones I wrote to you. I wrote you once a week."

I handed her a glass of wine and said, "I got no letters."

Her brows rose. "None at all?"

I shook my head.

"I know mail delivery is slow west of the Missouri, but I figured they would arrive sooner or later."

I shook my head again. "I didn't get one. I have to confess, at first I was hoping you would write. But as the weeks went by and none arrived..,"

"None arrived? What could have happened to them?"

Then the thought occurred to her. "I'll have to have a talk with Mother."

"Would she have intercepted the letters?

Why?"

"You don't know my mother. At least now I know why you never wrote me back."

She then said, "What did you possibly think? All that time with no contact from me?"

I shrugged. "I just thought maybe you might have put this place behind you. Me included."

She looked at me with a combination of sadness and disbelief. I am forever amazed at how women can combine emotions like that. "How could I ever put you behind me. What we had? What we have?"

I didn't know what to say. So I said nothing.

She said, "I'm so lucky that you didn't decide to move on. Find someone else. Or even worse, leave Wardtown."

"Maddie," I reached up and ran my hand through that incredible hair. "I could never move on. There is only you. There always has been only you, and there will always be only you."

Those were the magic words. She tossed her wine aside and the glass shattered on the floor and she wrapped her arms around me and her mouth was on mine again.

I did what any man in my position would do. I tossed my glass away and returned the kiss, which led to another and then another.

INTERLUDE
SAM WILSON

Sam stepped into the house with an armload of firewood. He had moved out of the house and back into the bunkhouse, but he figured he should at least make sure the wood box in the kitchen and the one in the parlor were filled.

He was hoping Amelia wouldn't be downstairs. The hour was late, and maybe she would have turned in. But to his disappointment, he saw her standing in the parlor, in front of the great stone hearth that he and Nathan Shannon had made. She was looking at the mantel, and the photographs Maddie had placed there. One of Nathan, and one of Maddie and Nathan standing together.

Sam remembered the day they had been taken. Back in the days before Jonathan Hooper's destructive reign in town had gotten out of hand. Nathan had brought in a photographer from Chicago and had some tintypes taken. Maddie and her father had stood in front of the hearth, holding ever so still while the photographer snapped his photo. The slightest motion could create a blurring effect on the picture. As such, they both looked stern and expressionless, which was the opposite of the way they actually were. Maddie was practically a wildcat. Always had been. And Nathan had an animated face with brows that rose or dropped, and he had always been quick with a grin. It was too bad such things were lost in a photograph.

Nathan had stood with his starched collar pressing tightly at his neck. He had kept his back ramrod straight. Maddie had stood beside him in an evening gown, one she had brought from St. Louis. The girl looked natural on the back of a horse, but she could make herself look elegant when she wanted to.

Sam remembered Nathan saying, "Will you take the picture already? I feel like I'm in a noose, with this collar."

Maddie had grinned.

The photographer said, "Hold still please. Both of you."

Nathan said, "Dadburn it, I'm trying."

Sam smiled at the memory, but the smile faded at the sight of the woman standing in front of the mantel.

She turned to face him. "Hello, Sam."

"Amelia," he said. "I was hoping you'd be upstairs."

"Oh, Sam. Is this the way it's going to be?"

Sam said nothing. He went to the wood box to dump the firewood.

"What?" she said. "You're not speaking to me?"

"Should I?"

"Sam." She shook her head and returned to the photographs on the mantel. "She looks good in these. Nathan did, too. But I still can't see why she would want to live her life here, in the middle of nowhere. She could have any man she wanted in St. Louis, or even Chicago. Fine young men of good breeding and with bright futures. Instead, she had to come running back to that cowboy marshal of hers."

Sam stood and brushed away the bits of debris you always get on yourself after carrying an armload of wood. "Austin Tremain is a good man."

"I'm sure he is. A straight-forward man. Probably exactly what that god-forsaken little town needs. But do you really want Madelyn marrying him? When she could have any one of the sons from any number of good families? Why, she could have a son who could be a senator."

"I don't think Maddie cares about that sort of thing. She's a cattlewoman at heart. This place is what she wants."

"Why can't she be interested in that doctor, in town? I met him. He seems like a genteel man. A man of education."

"Because her heart belongs to Tremain. That's the way of it."

Amelia gave a weary sigh. "I'm afraid you're right. She's not the first woman in our family to fall in love with a cowboy."

Sam turned away from her. He said, "We didn't hear from her at all the whole time she was gone, except for the letter saying she was coming home. I was starting to wonder if she would be coming back at all."

Amelia said, "I intercepted her letters, Sam."

Now he shot his gaze back to her, his eyes blazing. "You *what*?"

"I did what I thought was best. I was trying to help steer her future in a direction that would be better for her. A direction away from this place."

"There's nothing wrong with this place."

"It was wrong for me. It's wrong for her, too."

"You just want it to be wrong for her." Sam headed for the door. He grabbed it and pulled it open, then stopped as a thought occurred to him. A question. He looked back to her and said, "Did you tell her?"

"Of course not. What do you think I am?"

He again said nothing.

Amelia said, "Well, it's apparently obvious what you think of me. But it takes two to dance, Sam."

"I know. I live with it every day of my life. He was like a brother to me. He deserved better."

"Did you ever tell him?"

"No. He went to the grave not knowin'."

"Sam, Sam, Sam." She shook her head. "Are you ever going to learn to forgive yourself? I learned to forgive myself, long ago."

"I can't. I guess that's the difference between us."

He pulled open the door and was about to step out, but then stopped again.

He said, "She can't ever know."

"She'll never hear it from me. I know what it would do to the both of you."

Sam hesitated a moment, like there was more to say but he couldn't find the words. Finally, he just stepped out and into the night.

13

IT FELT LIKE MADDIE AND I WERE the only people on the entire planet. Like we were some sort of Adam and Eve. The wind howled outside the little sod cabin we were in, but we didn't care. Wrapped in each other's arms, a fire roaring in the stove, we fell off to sleep. I don't remember the last time I slept so peacefully.

Come morning, I went out to tend to the horses while Maddie made coffee, then she brought the coffee out and perched on a fence rail and I stood leaning one elbow against it.

As cold as the night before had been, the morning sun was warm, and I knew in just a few hours, the cold of the night would be long forgotten. The wind would hit you in the face with heat that would feel like an oven door had been opened.

Maddie was wearing only my shirt from the day before. This was a day and age when a woman never showed her legs except if she was dancing on a stage, and even then, those weren't the type of girls you would bring home to mother. But I found as she sat on the fence rail, Maddie's legs were better than those of any show girl I had ever seen.

I sipped at my coffee. Maybe it was the company, but I found it tastier even than Nell's.

Maddie and I had talked into the night. She had told me of the contents of her letters. And she told me how she had felt compelled to get away from the area where Jonathan Hooper had caused such destruction in her life and nearly driven her to murder. She had needed time away to find some sense of balance within herself.

"Well, he's gone," I said. "I saw to that myself. I witnessed the execution, and what's left of him is six feet under."

She told me of how her mother had tried to arrange a meeting between her and a man in town. A member of a prominent family. But she had said no. She told me she had only thoughts of me the entire time she was gone.

She sat on the fence rail, her bare knees together and the Texas wind in her hair. She held her coffee cup with both hands and took a sip.

I said, "I'm not a man of money. I have very little in the world. A woman like you deserves a proper engagement ring, and a man who can provide her with wealth and wonders."

She said, "I have everything I need in the world, right here. Right now."

"Then," I set my cup in the grass and got down on one knee and took her hand. "Madelyn Shannon, will you do me the honor of becoming my wife?"

She smiled the broadest, grandest smile I think anyone could ever muster.

She said, "As if there was every any doubt."

14

I STEPPED INTO my office to find Joe at my desk.

"Well," Joe said with a grin. "I was starting to think you two had run off and eloped."

"Is there any more coffee?"

Joe nodded, and swung a hand toward the stove standing in the corner. I went over and poured a cup.

I had ridden with Maddie to the ranch, and left her at the front porch. We had been gone two days, and since I was the town marshal, I figured the least I could do was check in with my office.

As Maddie had stood on the front porch of her ranch, I said, "You know, I probably should come in and meet your mother."

"That might not be a good idea. Not yet. I intend to ask her about those letters, and it could get a little loud in there. I would like to have you come out for dinner, but I'll let you know when."

Family politics. I understood. I had been blessed in that my family had little of this. My parents had been hardworking farmers. No dual agendas. Just going about their work, planting a crop and maintaining a household. And all the while, raising two boys. But most families weren't this blessed, and when money got involved like it did on Maddie's mother's side, things often got even more complicated.

The morning was a bit cool still, so I was glad to find the stove warming my little marshal's office. With a cup of coffee in hand, I sat at the edge of my desk.

"Funny you mentioned the word *elope*," I said to Joe. "We're getting married."

Joe shrugged. "We all know that."

"But I mean, I formally asked her. We just have to set a date. She wanted to talk to her mother, first."

"A complicated woman, I understand. Sam's not one to say much, but you can read it in him when you mention the woman's name."

I sat and drank my coffee, and Joe brought me up to date on town business.

Joe had broken up a scuffle at the saloon the night before. Nothing serious, just two cowhands with a little too much whiskey in them, swinging fists over a card game that had no more than three dollars on the table.

A new minister had arrived in town. A Revered What's-his-name. Joe couldn't remember. A middle-aged man. He was Methodist. We had a Methodist church here and they had sent a request for a pastor. They had been going without one for a while.

They could have just gone down the street to the Baptist church and listened to Eb preach, but it seemed to me church-going folks were sort of like the Union and the Confederacy during the War. You wouldn't expect Methodists to go to a Baptist church, or for Baptists to invite them. Would be like oil and water.

Folks at the Methodist church had been holding their own services even without a preacher, taking turns doing readings from the Good Book themselves. Since Doc Benson was an educated man, he had been asked to give a sermon, so one Sunday he spoke about how war was contrary to the teachings of Jesus, and I couldn't agree more.

And Jericho had put on a shooting exhibition the day before yesterday.

Joe said, "I went out to break it up. You don't want shooting exhibitions going on right in the street. But I wound up standing with my mouth hanging open. One feller would toss a silver dollar in the air, and then Jericho would jack his rifle and bring it to his shoulder and shoot a hole through the dollar before it could touch the ground. When he said he could do that, I thought he was exaggerating, but he did it again and again. He shot up nine dollars. A crowd gathered. Finally, I had to get in the act myself and threw two dollars in the air. Danged if he didn't get both of 'em."

Joe shook his head. "Only one I ever seen shoot like that was my brother. And he did it with a six-gun. Never seen anyone handle a rifle that fast."

I looked at the rifle rack and saw one was missing.

I said, "Jericho's keeping the rifle, I suppose."

Joe shrugged. "Might as well. He's someone you want armed, in case you need help in a hurry."

I took a sip of my coffee. "Wants to be a lawman. But he's all elbows and knees. Almost trips over his own feet."

"Not with that rifle, he don't."

"You think he'll ever be a lawman?"

Joe said, "He's got the heart for it. Yeah, I think he'll do. I think he's gonna turn into a man to ride the river with."

SAM RODE INTO town that afternoon. But he didn't come to the marshal's office like he usually did. He went straight to the saloon.

I only knew he was in town because Joe knew I was waiting for a dinner invitation from Maddie, and Joe came in and told me Sam was here.

"That's strange," I said.

"Yeah. I figured he was here to tell you when to belly up at the Shannon table."

I got to my feet. My gunbelt was rolled up on my desk, so I grabbed it and strapped it on. I didn't bother to tie it down, though. This town was so different than it had been when I first rode in a year ago, so quiet and peaceful, you would have thought it was an entirely different part of the country.

I found Sam at the bar. One foot on the railing, one elbow on the bar and a glass in his hand. The glass was empty and so he set it down on the bar, and the barkeep tipped a bottle over it and refilled it.

Apparently he had walked in and immediately knocked one back.

"Sam," I said.

He glanced over at me. "Tremain."

He then took a plug of the whiskey.

"Washing down the trail dust?" I said.

"Somethin' like that."

I stopped at the bar and nodded at the barkeep. "Why don't you give me a beer, Ned."

Sam said, "Too early for whiskey?"

I shrugged. "I *am* on duty."

"This town's so quiet these days, the marshal

could go away for an entire week and I don't think anyone would notice."

"Sam, what's eating you?"

Sam shook his head and then just stood there, staring at the bar. This was not one of the fancier saloons you might see in a place like San Francisco. There was no mirror behind the bar, no painting of any half-dressed woman reclining back in a lounge. Just wooden planks nailed upright, and a wooden shelf that held a few whiskey bottles. There were two beer kegs on the floor, both with taps on them. One from St. Louis, and one from Milwaukee.

"You ever do somethin' you wish you hadn't done?" Sam said.

I thought about that for moment. "I suppose we all have, one way or another."

"Well, this is a big one. And it's one I can't never talk about."

Sam knocked back another mouthful of whiskey, then he said, "Oh, by the way, you're invited out to the ranch tomorrow night. Dinner with Maddie and her mother. That's what I was actually sent to town to do. Give you the invitation."

He reached into his vest and pulled out a small envelope and handed it to me.

"What's this?" I said.

"The invitation, I guess."

I opened the envelope and pulled out a folded sheet of granulated paper. I had never seen such a thing. Written on it, in an almost impossibly flourish, were the words:

You are cordially invited to dinner with myself and my daughter Madelyn. Cocktails will be at 7:00.

And it was signed *Amelia McAllister Shannon*.

I remembered Maddie had told me that her parents lived apart for most of her life, but they had never divorced.

In the bottom corner were the letters *RSVP*. I asked Sam what that meant.

He shrugged. "Danged if I know."

And that was all he said. He went back to staring off into space.

I hated to see Sam all torn up this way. But here in the West, it was our way not to prod a man with questions. If he wanted to talk, you listened. But once he said all he was going to say, you let it go at that.

I stood beside Sam and sipped at my beer. He leaned against the bar on his elbows, his glass of whiskey in front of him, and stared off into nothingness.

15

I HAD never been one for dressing up. With my collar buttoned tight and a tie wrapped around my neck, I felt like I was standing on a gallows.

I normally wore jeans. In fact, the only pants I owned were jeans. I managed to find a pair of charcoal gray, pinstriped trousers at the general store that might be a little more fitting for dinner at the Shannon Ranch, but I had no jacket, and there were none at the store that were within my meager price range. Then Doc Benson offered to let me wear one of his.

The jacket was also a dark gray and pinstriped. It almost matched the trousers.

Doc said, "In the light of day, the color is close but doesn't quite entirely match. But in the dimmer light of a candelabra, the jacket'll do."

I shook my head. I was standing in his office with the jacket on. He was a tad taller than I was and his shoulders had struck me as being a little wider, but maybe they weren't because the jacket seemed to fit just about right.

I said, "I've been out there to eat a number of times. But tonight, because of that woman out there, I'll feel like I'm stepping into hostile territory. And I'll be armed with only a tie and a jacket."

Doc grinned. His own jacket was off. He was in a white shirt and a vest, and a string tie. Most strong men struck me as feeling a little confined in such clothes, but he seemed comfortable.

He said, "I met Amelia the other day."

"Amelia?" I said. "You're on a first-name

basis with her?"

He shrugged. "She was in town. She told me to call her Amelia. The thing with people like that is they are all about the show. They don't care how much substance a man has, they are only concerned about how he presents himself. And how much money he has in the bank."

"If it had been folks like that who first came to Texas, this land would still belong to the Comanche."

He grinned. "Indeed."

I had noticed Doc Benson very seldom laughed. He usually just grinned. But when he did laugh, it was a down-deep belly laugh that would cause him to almost fall over.

I said, "I can't believe that woman gave me a hand-written invitation. Like I was some sort of high-society dude out of San Francisco or St. Louis."

"It's just her way."

"Do you know what the initials *RSVP* mean?"

He nodded with another grin. "It means they want you to indicate whether or not you'll be accepting the invitation. It comes from the French, *respondez, s'il vous plait*. Respond, if you please."

"How do you know all this stuff?"

He shrugged. "I have a varied and sundry background. I'm afraid if you knew half of it, you would want to arrest me."

I waved the suggestion away with my hand, like I was swatting a fly. The Doc was a stand-up man. That's all I needed to know. Just like with Sam at the bar, you didn't prod a man for information.

I said, "It should be obvious that I'll be there. Anytime Maddie asks me there for dinner, I'll be there. It's a given."

"With people like Amelia McAllister, it's all about the show. The song and dance."

I stood in front of a full-length mirror that was against one wall. I looked at myself in the dress trousers and Doc's jacket. I looked downright ridiculous.

"I'll never be able to impress that woman," I said. "I can't do the song if I don't know the words. I can't do the dance if I don't know the steps. And I have no money in any bank. The change in my pocket is all I have for my life's savings."

"You'll do all right. Just follow my lead."

I looked at him.

He said, "I'm afraid I'll be there, too. The good lady McAllister sent an invitation to me, too. I have absolutely no idea why. The last thing I want is to have to sit at a table with people like that and play their game. This is one thing I was hoping to avoid out here in Texas."

"But you accepted?"

He shrugged. "I tried to think of an excuse. I was grasping at straws."

"Can't you just say *no thanks*?"

He shook his head. "Not with those people. In a place like St. Louis, I could simply let it go that I was *otherwise engaged*. But in this town, she'll know there are no other dinners or soirees of any kind. She would know I just didn't want to be there. I don't need to get on the wrong side of a person like that. They can be ruthless in trying to ruin a person."

I thought about what Maddie had said. She had written me letters that her mother intercepted.

I said, "Maddie described her as devious."

"Like I said, they care nothing for character. It's all about presentation and money."

I looked at myself in the mirror again. "I'm afraid I'm not going to do too well on presentation."

Doc got to his feet and slapped me on the shoulder. "All you need to do is focus your attention on Miss Shannon. From what I saw in the street the other day, when she ran to you, you two have the kind of love that most of us can only dream about finding. Ultimately, it doesn't matter what her mother thinks. It only matters what Miss Shannon thinks."

I went back to my office and sat down behind my desk. I was still in my new dress pants, but I had taken off the jacket.

I thought I could use a cup of coffee, but the stove was standing cold and the day was too warm for me to go heating it up. I thought maybe I might walk down to the restaurant for a cup.

Then my gaze landed on the stack of reward posters on my desk. The stack that I, as town marshal, was supposed to go through and then tack up on the wall outside. And I remembered something Doc Benson had said. If I knew his story, I might want to arrest him.

I thought of going through those posters. I wondered if I would find him in there. Or maybe someone going by a different name but that would match his description.

This is the part about being a law officer that is maybe the hardest. Having to play judge and jury. They say a lawman just upholds the law and leaves the judging to the courts. But that ain't really the way of it. You see, lawmen are human, too. Doc Benson was an unusual combination of things. A doctor, an educated man who spoke with a theatrical flair and who understood the ways of high society, and yet had shoulders like a man who belonged swinging an axe, and wore his revolver like a gunfighter. But he had proven himself to be a good man, and was becoming a friend.

I left the stack of posters where they were, grabbed the jacket and headed down to Nell's for that coffee.

16

LATER ON, AFTER I HAD returned to my office, Joe and Jericho laughed at me when they saw me in the white shirt and string tie, and my new dress pants and Doc's jacket.

Joe said, "Well, now, you look fit to preach a sermon."

He was sitting at my desk. Jericho was perched on the edge of the desk, his Winchester leaning within reach.

"Laugh all you want," I said.

"Oh, we are."

Jericho's hair was as bushy as the mop he pushed down at the saloon. His face was thin and he had whiskers that were fine as corn silk. Pinned to his shirt was a tin star.

He said, "I just gotta say, Marshal, I'm glad it's you goin' and not me. I don't know what I'd say at a fine dinner like what you got waitin' ahead of you."

I said, "Doc's been coaching me on how to eat something called *hors d'oerves*. Some sort of food they serve before they serve the real meal."

I shook my head. "It's some sort of French word. Seems with these folks, everything has to be in French. I guess it sounds fancier than English."

Jericho said, "Give me a steak and potatoes down at Nell's, any day."

"Same for me, as long as Maddie is there with me."

Joe said, "And that's the crux of it right there. Just remember, you're doin' this for Maddie."

I reached for my gunbelt and buckled it on. I said, "I don't know how Doc wears a gun with pants like these. My gunbelt keeps sliding down."

Joe chuckled. "I don't think you're supposed to wear a gun to a fine dinner."

I unbuckled the belt and dropped it to my desk. "I don't know. Goin' all that way, unarmed."

"Here." Joe reached to his holster and pulled out a gun. He had taken to wearing his pistol on his left side since his shooting hand got all torn up by a bullet the summer before.

The gun he handed me was a Colt, like my own, but it was shorter barreled.

Joe said, "I always used a shorter barrel. Gave me an edge in a fast draw. But it don't do me much good now. I rely on a scattergun, these days. Don't know why I carry a pistol at all. You take it. It might fit in your jacket pocket."

I slipped the gun into the pocket. It did fit, but it was heavy and pulled at the jacket. Then I tried it in my trouser pocket, and it was perfect fit. My own pistol, with a seven and a half inch barrel, would have been a little long.

"Thanks, Joe."

The door opened and in stepped Doc. He looked dapper as always. A dark gray jacket and trousers, a checkered vest, a string tie. I noticed he wasn't wearing a gun, either.

He said, "I'm glad you haven't left yet. I was thinking maybe we could ride out together. Misery loves company."

I said, "Why do I feel like we're going to be riding into a rattler's nest?"

"Because, my friend, we are."

17

MADDIE WAS in an evening gown that fell just off the shoulder, with Spanish style lace around the neckline. Her hair was all done up in some sort of do that looked like she had tamed the ocean and was somehow holding it in place.

When you love a woman, no matter how many times you look at her it's like seeing her beauty for the first time. This was how I felt looking at her now. I tried not to stand with my mouth hanging open, like a school boy seeing a woman for the first time.

She gave me a quick peck on the cheek. "I'm so glad you could make it."

I said, "I'm so sorry I didn't *RSVP*."

I glanced quickly at Doc, and he gave a subtle nod of his head. I had used the term correctly.

Maddie was giving me a smile that all but took my breath away. The kind of a smile a woman only fixes on the man she loves.

She said, "You didn't have to RSVP. I knew you were coming, because we belong at each other's side."

I then said, "Allow me to introduce Doctor Thomas Benson."

She held out her hand and he grasped it lightly. She said, "I'm so pleased to make your acquaintance, Doctor Benson."

"Please," he said, "Call me Doc. All of my friends do."

Maddie then took my hand. "Come. It's time for you to meet Mother."

Doc said quietly, "Here we go. Into the lion's den."

Maddie gave a quick giggle.

Amelia McΛllister Shannon stood in the center of the parlor. She stood as though the entire world revolved around her. Maybe in her mind, it did.

"Mother," Maddie said, "allow me to introduce the town marshal and my fiancé, Austin Tremain."

She stood a moment. I stood. Neither of us moved.

Doc had given me some coaching the afternoon before. One thing he told me is you don't reach for a woman's hand to shake it, like you would with a man. If she offers her hand, you take it lightly, like he had with Maddie. If she doesn't offer her hand, then you don't reach for it.

Finally, she did. I grasped it lightly.

"I am so pleased to make your acquaintance, ma'am," I said.

I hated lying—it didn't set well with me at all. I was not at all pleased to meet this woman. She was Maddie's mother, but intercepting those letters was something that would always be between her and me. Treachery like that could get a man shot, out here in the West.

She raised a brow at me, and said, "Charmed, I'm sure."

I said, "I'm sure."

Doc grinned. Maddie turned away and brought a hand to her mouth to hold back another giggle.

Maddie then introduced Doc.

"We have met," her mother said. "While you and the good marshal were off having your little soiree."

To Doc, she said, "I'm so glad you could be here tonight, doctor."

I noticed he didn't tell her to call him Doc. A subtle way of saying she was not his friend. I was beginning to notice these high-society affairs were filled with subtleties.

"Would you all join me for hor d'oerves?" the old bat said. "And maybe some cocktails?"

As she walked away, Maddie grasped both of my hands and said, "Austin, that was great."

Doc slapped me on the shoulder. "My friend, that was the classiest thing I've seen anyone do in a long time. In her world, she was raising the stakes and you called her bluff."

A Mexican woman I had never seen before came from the kitchen.

"Esmerelda, I would like a glass of sherry," Amelia said and looked to her daughter. "Madelyn?"

Maddie said to me, "We have a bottle of Kentucky bourbon."

I couldn't help but grin. "A glass of that would set right nicely. Thank you."

Doc said, "Likewise, if I may."

"Mother," Maddie said, "I'll be joining our guests with a glass of bourbon."

Amelia shot her daughter a look that said she was not at all pleased.

Sam was milling about. He was still in his range shirt, but had buttoned the top button and was wearing a string tie. He came over.

I said, "How'd you get roped into this?"

He said, "I live here, remember? I couldn't get out of it."

Maddie said, "Come on, you two. For dinner with my mother, I want as much support around me as I can get."

Doc said with a grin, "Strength in numbers?"

She nodded. "You understand perfectly."

I took an hor d'oerve in one hand and bit into it. The old lady was watching me, like she was waiting for me to say something wrong or do something wrong, or drop a crumb on the floor.

I held a napkin under it as I bit into the thing. Tasted like something scraped up from a cow pasture, but what I said was, "Exquisite."

Maddie smiled with surprise. I don't think she expected such a word out of me. Even Sam, despite his foul mood, managed to twitch his mustache in a sort of half-grin.

Doc held a straight face, but his eyes were shining with a smile, and he gave me a barely perceptible nod of his head. He had coached me well. He had said when eating with people like this, you never say, *this sure tastes good*, or *mmm-boy that hit the spot.* You use words like *Exquisite. Elegant. Scrumptious.*

I had said, "Scrumptious? What kind of word is that? French?"

He nodded. "Might as well be."

It struck me a little odd, as I watched Doc navigate the tricky social waters of this high-society style gathering, that he could do this so well but seemed to have little respect for it.

When we sat for dinner, I made sure that I was just a beat behind Doc the whole way. At this table, you didn't tuck your napkin into the front of your shirt. You left it folded neatly on one knee. And you didn't wipe your mouth with it. You dabbed at your lips. I followed Doc's lead all the way. I watched which fork he used when the salad came out.

Old Lady McAllister served a roast covered with some sort of fancy yellowish sauce dumped all over it. There was a French name for it that I decided not to even waste my time trying to remember. I will admit, the roast was cooked rare and would have been downright tasty if not for that yellowish goo.

From this point onward, my advice to anyone cooking is to not dump yellow goo on your beef.

Old Lady McAllister had tried to embarrass me just before dinner was served by asking me if I would like, as the guest, to select the wine.

Doc had asked Sam to look at the wine collection the old lady had brought with her.

"Just a bunch of Italian and French words," Sam had said.

Doc asked him to write them down.

Doc found out from Sam that the old lady would be serving "some sort of damned beef dish."

So Doc coached me in that, too.

I said, with all eyes on me, "I think tonight's dinner would call for something full bodied. Say, a Syrrah."

This got a smile of surprise from the old lady. She had a Mexican man serving as her butler—the same one who had ridden on the top of the stage. She had him pull the cork out of the bottle, then he poured just a smidgen in my wine glass. The old lady was watching me to see me slip up. But I picked up the glass and gave it a sniff. *Testing the ambiance*, is the term. Doc didn't need to coach me in this part of the dance. I had seen it done at an officer's dinner back during the late War Betwixt the States.

After the sniff, I nodded approvingly, as if there was something in the smell of the wine that was somehow pleasing. I then took a sip and sat thoughtfully for a moment.

I then said, "Indeed. This will more than suffice."

The Mexican man then filled the old lady's glass, then Maddie's, then he got the rest of us. He was a man of about fifty who seemed well-versed in the doings of the high-society folk, though he spoke broken English with a thick Mexican accent. He answered to the name Julio.

The old lady didn't even look at him as he filled her glass. Like he was somehow part of the furniture. But when he came to me, I decided that holding my own with the old lady was one thing, but being rude was something else entirely.

I looked the man in the eye and said, "Gracias, Senor."

He allowed me a quick smile and a nod of his head.

I found the wine tasted like cough syrup, but everyone else at the table seemed to be find it pleasing.

According to Doc, folks at these shindigs didn't actually eat. They nibbled at their food. They took a tiny amount on a fork and nibbled it down, then they made conversation. They never just dug into their meal like they were hungry. So this is what I did. I followed Doc's lead, and the smiles Maddie was giving me, a mixture of apology and relief, told me I was doing the dance right.

Doc told me to watch out for any pointed questions. They might come at me from the side, or it might be a head-on attack.

At dinner, Old Lady McAllister decided to take the head-on approach.

"So, Marshal Tremain," she said, "if I may be so bold, what are your career plans?"

Maddie shot her mother a glance that was not friendly. The old expression *if looks could kill* applied to this very moment.

I dabbed at my mouth with my napkin and said, "Well, the ranches in the area all pay this week, so I'm expecting Saturday night to be a real hootenanny. So I'll have my guns loaded and the coffee pot hot. I'll have Jericho on duty, and maybe Joe," I looked at Sam, "if you can spare him."

Sam said, "Any time you need him."

The old lady allowed a reluctant smile. "And what are your plans beyond Saturday?"

"Sunday morning, I plan to go listen to the new preacher in town. I also plan on asking Maddie to join me." I glanced at Maddie and she flashed me another smile. I said, "In the afternoon, I'll probably walk my rounds, get a cup of coffee, and then try to get caught up on some paperwork that I've been managing to avoid for a few weeks."

The old lady was clearly not amused. She

said, "Have you no plans for the future at all?"

Maddie said, "Mother."

I decided to say what I thought I should say, not necessarily what the old lady would expect one of her high-society friends to say.

I said, "Ma'am, when I was in the war, I saw a lot of good men killed. Some of them were friends. When I got back home after the war, I found my family gone. I learned to live each day and find the beauty in it, and not to put too much stock in tomorrow because tomorrow might never get here."

"But surely one must plan for the future."

"I am surrounded by good people." I glanced from Maddie to Sam to Doc. "I work in a small town that's filled with good people. I do a job that I'm good at. I may not earn a lot of money, but I'm happy."

The old lady looked down at the plate in front of her. Nothing more was said. But I was sure I hadn't heard the last of it.

18

AFTER DINNER, MADDIE AND STEPPED
outside. She had a goblet of syrrah in her hand, and I
had another glass of bourbon. We stood on the porch
that faced the barn. She had one hand hooked into the
crook of my arm.

She said, "You handled Mother beautifully at
dinner."

"I scouted for the Apache for a couple of
years. I faced outlaws once when I was riding shotgun
for a stage company. One time I rode into Mexico
chasing after border raiders who had kidnapped a girl.
I never knew that all of this was actually training for
tonight's dinner."

She laughed.

She said, "Mother means well. At least I hope
she does. But she has a different set of principles than
I do."

We stepped down off the porch. It was dark,
but the sky above was clear and a three-quarter moon
was lighting things up right nicely.

Maddie said, "Mother so desperately wants
me to pursue Doctor Benson, you know."

I hadn't known this. I wasn't surprised,
though.

Maddie said, "I told her my heart belonged to
you."

"I'll bet she didn't like hearing that."

Maddie chuckled. "Let's just say we had an
interesting afternoon."

I said, "They say the apple doesn't fall far
from the tree. How is it you're so different from your

mother?"

"I suppose you could say my apple didn't fall far from my father's tree. My father was very different than my mother. When I first started coming to this ranch when I was a child, something about it seemed to connect to something inside me. I knew I was home. And it wasn't just the land or the cattle or the horses, or this incredible house Father and Sam built. It was the people. Father and Sam, especially, but also the ranchers in the area. Texas folk. There is something so incredibly real about them. I began coming out here every summer, and once I turned eighteen, I came here to live."

She had told me this before, but it all took on a different light now that I had met her mother.

I said, "What did your mother say about you moving out here?"

"Of course, she wasn't happy. But she had to admit that I was much more like Father than like her. I finally said to her that she has to stop trying to make me into the daughter she wished she had."

"Ouch," I said. As much as the old lady had ticked me off, I had to admit hearing this probably stung a little.

"Well, she needed to hear it. Things have been a little frosty between us ever since, but they were fairly frosty before that, anyway. Mother is not a warm person. Never affectionate. As the sole heir to her family's fortune, she is actually quite powerful. Maybe she felt she needed to be cold in order to be strong. She might irk me every so often—quite a lot, actually—but all in all, I feel sorry for her."

I had never been one to think much about

material possessions. Investments and wealth and such. I had been raised on a farm. In the years since the war, I had been roaming the West going from one job to another. I am good at tracking, and was always a good shot with a gun and good with my fists. Combine that with the experience I got in the war, and I was ideal for jobs such as scouting for the Army or riding shotgun, or riding for the Texas Rangers. I never put much thought in needing anything more than a good horse beneath me, some supplies in my saddle bags, and maybe a pistol at my side and a rifle in my saddle. Good drinking water in my canteen.

To me, sharing coffee with some friends was what I considered quality time. Or passing a whiskey bottle back and forth around a campfire. Laughing and telling tall tales. Making memories you can carry with you for a lifetime.

But Maddie was a prominent businesswoman in this part of Texas. She owned this entire ranch. A couple thousand head of cattle. Sam was the ramrod of this place, and he worked for her. I thought of Joe as working for Sam, but actually he worked for Maddie. Come Saturday night when cowhands would descend on my little town, almost one in four of them would be on Maddie's payroll. And her mother apparently owned a sizeable fortune and lived in a mansion that was practically a small palace in St. Louis. I knew Maddie was an only child, which meant she would probably one day inherit all of it.

I realized for the really the first time that Maddie was a rich woman. Successful. Potentially powerful, herself. And me, I was a lawman. A former Army scout. A former cowhand. She owned all the land about us, literally as far as the eye could see. And I owned little more than the clothes on my back. Even the jacket I wore was borrowed from Doc Benson.

"What're you thinking about?" she said.

"Us."

She smiled. "Hopefully good thoughts."

Actually, I was finding they were uncertain thoughts. But before I could say anything, I saw Sam Wilson standing out back in the moonlight. I was kind of glad, because I wasn't really sure what I was thinking.

I said, "What's Sam doing out there?"

She followed my gaze. "That's Juan's grave."

We walked over. The wooden grave marker still stood.

We stood beside Sam. Maddie sort of snuggled into me, and I put my arm around her.

Maddie said, "He was like a brother to me."

The grave marker read JUAN SHANNON.

Sam said, "He sure earned that name. He paid for it with his blood."

I nodded. One more reminder of the legacy of Jonathan Hooper.

"I plan to have a marble headstone made," Maddie said, "and shipped out here."

Sam said, "I come out here once nearly every day. Pay Juan a visit. Talk to him about ranch business."

Maddie said, "Are you all right, Sam? You've seemed a bit out of sorts for the past few days."

"Oh, it's just..," he shrugged and waved it off.

"It's Mother, isn't it?"

He sighed, and nodded. "I suppose I should have known what to expect. I know what she's like. I even moved back out to the bunk house, thinking it might be easier."

"Sam, you're like a father to me. I hope you know that."

He looked over at her. I saw his eyes were glistening.

He said, "Punkin, you're like a daughter to me. Always will be."

Sam still had that way about him. That edginess that comes from feeling really angry or sad about something, but holding it in. The same way he had been at the saloon.

I wanted to tell Sam if he should ever decide to talk about it that I was there for him. But Sam was a strong man, a man of the frontier, and such men were often embarrassed by their own strong feelings, and even more embarrassed if people were aware of them. So instead, I just clamped a hand on his shoulder and we all stood silently for a while looking down at Juan's grave.

19

DOC AND I STARTED back to town at about ten o'clock that night. As much as I hated to part company with Maddie, I was relieved to be away from Amelia McAllister Shannon.

I said, "I'll bet the city of Saint Louis was relieved when that woman announced she was coming out to Texas to visit."

Doc laughed. "I'll bet they were."

Doc had pulled his gunbelt from his saddle bags and strapped it on before he swung into the saddle. I decided not to bother. These trousers were too slippery for a gunbelt. I would just ride with the short-barreled revolver Joe had loaned me in my trouser pocket.

Doc said, "You did really well back there, I hope you know. You handled this evening like a veteran."

"You know, Maddie told me her mother wants her to focus her attention on you."

Doc shook his head. "Even if she wasn't spoken for by a good friend, I would have to say no. Her mother represents a lifestyle I left behind and want no part of. I have set my sights on another."

This had me guessing.

When we arrived in town, he said, "I'll stop at your office with you. I have something in there waiting for the both of us."

We left our horses at the livery and walked the length of boardwalk to my office. I found the lantern burning and Joe asleep on the bunk.

The stove was burning low and was warm,

and on the top were two pans of food each covered with a cloth.

Doc said, "I had Nell bring these by the office. I asked her to do so about nine."

I lifted one cloth. There was a steak in the pan and some mashed potatoes oozing with butter, and some squash. And a home-made biscuit.

Doc said, "I'm always hungry when I leave one of those ridiculous dinners. I thought you would be, too."

We took the chair behind my desk and dove into my second dinner of the night. My first real one. Doc sat at one corner of my desk and started doing the same.

I said, "Nell, huh?"

He grinned. "A good woman. Solid. Upstanding. And real. So incredibly real."

I nodded. "She is all of that. And a great cook."

"Indeed," he said, and bit into his biscuit.

20

IKE HAWKINS OF THE TEXAS RANGERS rode down the length of the town's main street and swung out of the saddle in front of my office. I was at my desk actually looking at my ledger sheet. Joe was there, too. He had ridden into town from the Shannon Ranch for morning coffee.

I heard the rider out front, and looked out the window and saw it was Hawkins. I hadn't seen him since he and his men delivered Hooper to us weeks ago.

I stepped onto the boardwalk while he was giving his horse's rein a couple of turns around the hitching rail.

"Hawkins," I said.

"Tremain. Good to see you."

"I got some coffee on if you want to come in."

He followed me back into the office, and I indicated Joe with a wave of my hand, and said, "Joe Smith. One of my deputies."

Hawkins shook Joe's hand and said, "I remember. Good to see you."

He took a wooden upright chair in front of my desk, and I filled two tin cups from a pot on the stove and handed one to him. I had let the fire in the stove go out and the coffee was cooling down, but it was still coffee. On the frontier, a man learns to live on coffee because the water often isn't fit to drink unless you boil it first.

I went back to my chair and sat down.

"Passing through?" I said.

He shook his head. "Captain McNelly sent

me. Got some news you need to hear. It's about Jonathan Hooper."

I felt a wave of exasperation come over me, and I'll admit it showed.

Hawkins said, "You probably thought you'd heard the last of that name."

"I was hoping."

Joe shook his head and said through his thick beard, "That name's like a bad penny. Keeps turnin' up."

Hawkins took a sip of his coffee. "Have you ever heard the name Ambrose Conrad?"

I shook my head. I glanced over at Joe, and he shook his head.

Hawkins said, "He's a mercenary, and an assassin. They say he's as bad as they come. He was in the War Betwixt the States, riding with some guerilla raiders in Kansas and Missouri. Then he started hiring out his gun to various places throughout the world. Mexico. South America, even. He uses various names. They had him in a Mexican prison for a time. A place with no name. It doesn't officially exist, but Captain McNelly has scouted the place. They keep political prisoners there, and prisoners they don't want the world to know about. Near a town called El Rosario."

I nodded. I had heard of it. I glanced over to Joe again, and he said, "They call it The Pit."

Hawkins said, "That's the place. The Mexicans threw him in there for a while, but then they let him out because they had a job for him to do. No one knows what it was, but it couldn't have been very nice. But then he escaped from them."

Joe said, "I don't mean to be rude, but how does any of this involve us, or Hooper?"

"He's Jonathan Hooper's half-brother."

Joe shook his head. "Like a bad penny."

I said, "What's he look like?"

Hawkins said, "That's the rub of it. No one knows. They say he's like a human chameleon. He can change his looks by shaving a beard or growing one. By carrying himself a little different."

"Does McNelly think he might come here?"

"We heard about the thing Hooper said to you all a couple of times before he was hanged. And we were told the name the Mexicans have for this man. *Angel Vengador.*

I knew enough Spanish to know what this meant. I looked at Joe and said, "The Avenging Angel."

PART FOUR
THE AVENGING ANGEL

21

HAWKINS RODE on. He had a lot of miles to cover before nightfall. But the news he had delivered left Joe and me with a lot to think about.

We stood on the boardwalk in front of the office, looking at the town before us.

I said, "I'm gonna ride back out to the ranch with you, to tell Maddie about all of this."

"Do you really think this Conrad feller will come here, looking for trouble?"

"Hooper seemed to think so. Maybe they had been in contact, somehow."

"And the thing is, apparently no one knows what he looks like."

"We need to be careful about strangers coming into town. Check them out carefully. When the stage arrives, one of us needs to be on hand. We shouldn't make it look obvious, but just be on hand. Anyone who looks suspicious, we should check out. Also, I'm going to ride out to the surrounding ranches and see if they've hired any new hands in the past few weeks. Even though I have no jurisdiction out there as town marshal, I do as a Texas Ranger. I may be on indefinite leave, but I still have the authority."

Then I said, "I'm gonna ask Sam for your services for a while."

"I doubt there'll be any problem there."

After a moment, Joe said, "I could use another cup of coffee, but that coffee in your pot is getting cold."

"One of us could start another fire in the stove."

He shook his head. "That little office will heat up like a furnace, and the day's already too hot for that. Let's go down to Nell's."

We did. She had coffee ready and her face was a little flushed from the heat of her own stove out in the kitchen, but you didn't feel the heat in the dining room. Even still, Joe and I took our coffee outside.

We stood on the boardwalk. It was getting hot outdoors, but the air was dry and the wind steady. Every so often the wind would change direction and a gust would sweep down the street, sending dust and small pebbles scattering.

Joe said, "You gotta figure what the man's motivation would be. Revenge for his brother. My brother Johnny said one time if you want to outthink your opponent, you first have to figure out what he's gonna do. And the best way to do that is to put yourself in his place."

I nodded. "My commanding officer in the War said the same thing once."

"Seems to me, if I was in his place, my two main targets would be you and Maddie. Maybe in that order. You're the one who arrested Hooper, but with a lot of help from her. Or he might be targeting just you. But either way, maybe we should approach it that way. Abe Taggart might be a target too, because he turned on Hooper, but he should be safe because he's not here. I don't think anyone has heard from him since he rode out."

"Maddie and Sam will have to post pickets at night. They'll have to watch for any riders approaching the house."

Joe took a sip of coffee and wiped his mouth with the back of his sleeve. I had a little internal chuckle imagining how Maddie's mother would like seeing that.

Joe said, "It'll be a lot like it was, back when Hooper was still here."

"Maddie's gonna hate that."

Joe was wearing his pistol again, turned around to his left side, but he hadn't brought his scatter gun. I guess he figured he was just riding into town for coffee, not fixing to wage war again.

I said, "You might want to keep your scatter gun with you."

He nodded. "I might even borry that one from your office for the ride back to the ranch, if'n you don't mind."

"That sounds like a good idea," I said. I figured if you have a McCabe riding with you, you wanted him able to shoot.

He said, "You know, I just had me a thought."

I waited. Joe wasn't a man of many words, and if you prodded him along, you wouldn't get anywhere.

He said, "You ain't gonna like it."

I waited.

He said, "What if this Angel of Death feller is here right now?"

I looked at him. I didn't quite follow what he was saying.

He said, "Hawkins said he could change his

106

looks just by cutting his hair or shaving his beard, or growing one. They say he could carry himself different. I've seen actors like that, back east. Change the way they walk, put on a little disguise, and they can play a totally different character than the way they really are. What if he's here right now. In town."

"You're right," I said. "I don't like the sound of that. I wouldn't even know where to start looking."

I found myself glancing up and down the empty street. As I was looking, the door to Doc Benson's office opened, and he stepped out. He saw us and threw a wave at us and started walking over.

"I hate to say it," Joe said. "He seems like a good man. But I think I'd start looking right there."

22

MADDIE WAS in a gray split skirt and riding boots. A white blouse and a matching gray vest. Her hair was tied up in a bun behind her head.

She stood at the desk in the little nook off of her parlor that served as an office, and slammed her fist into it.

"Damn," she said. "It's starting all over again."

Joe and I had just delivered the news.

Sam stood nearby, a cigar smoldering away in his hand. "Ambrose Conrad, huh?"

I nodded. "A half-brother."

The old woman had a sense that she wasn't quite welcome. That this circle of four had gone to war together, and there was a bond between us that you just couldn't quite crack unless you had been part of it. But she drifted over toward us, anyway.

She said, "Maddie, you told me about this Hooper person. Was it really as bad as you say?"

Sam shot her a glance, then looked away. I could sense true animosity on his part toward her. But she just gave him a sad glance.

"What are we going to do?" She said.

Sam said nothing. Maddie stood, her fist now resting on her desk. She was just shaking her head and saying nothing. I suppose she was the one who had been the most affected by Hooper. And me—I didn't want to say anything to the old woman. Ever.

It was Joe, the man of few words, who spoke. He said, "We're gonna handle it. Just like we did with his brother."

Joe fetched his scatter gun from the bunkhouse and tucked some clothes in his bedroll, and we started back for town. Joe was like me, in that he owned very little other than the horse beneath him and the clothes on his back. Even the scatter gun had originally come from the rifle racks in Maddie's house.

Joe rode with the gun across his saddle horn. Sam had told me I could have Joe as long as I needed him, and he said to Joe, "Here, you might need this too," and tossed him a Winchester. Joe rode with the Winchester tucked into his saddle.

Joe had ridden out with the scatter gun from my office. I now had that one in my own saddle boot.

I wasn't about to criticize a McCabe, but I wondered how much good Joe's scatter gun would do on the ride back to town. The land about us was all open. It looked flat at first glance, but it was actually made up of long, low hills that stretched out almost flat, but not quite. They were covered with dry, brown grass. A sniper out there could get a shot at us, if he was hidden well, but he would be well beyond scatter gun range. So I rode with my rifle across my own saddle horn.

My rifle wasn't a Winchester, but a Spencer. It was a repeater and you jacked one cartridge into the chamber at a time, just like with a Winchester. The difference was the magazine wasn't under the barrel like with a Winchester, but in the stock. I had seen a Spencer one time take a bullet to the stock and the cartridges in the magazine all exploded, killing the man. One of the drawbacks of a Spencer. But found the gun more solidly built, less likely to jam, and better balanced.

Spencers had been out of production for a few years now, but a gunsmith had set up shop in town over the past winter, and I found this one there. Gunpowder has a way of corroding the life out of a gun bore, but this one was in good shape. My office budget was too tight for me to buy it, so I instead traded one of the Winchesters the town had provided for me. I didn't know if I was authorized to do that, but I figured I would give it a try, and so far no one had complained.

As we rode, I said to Joe, "Why do you suspect Doc?"

"Look at him. A man of contradictions. A doctor, but he looks more like a professional fighter. He carries his gun like a gunfighter. He rides his horse like he's born to it. You don't learn none of that at medical school. And have you taken a good look at his hands? He's got scar tissue on his knuckles. You don't get that by setting broken bones and deliverin' babies. You get that by punching a man. And his nose has been broke at least once."

"All right. So he's a man of mystery."

"And right now, any man of mystery is someone worth watching close."

23

ONCE THE SEEDS OF DOUBT ARE planted, they seem to grow on their own.

I made a cup of coffee, and since it was too warm to sit in my office with the stove burning, I went out and sat on an upright chair I had placed on the boardwalk near my office door.

A day had passed since Joe and I had ridden out to the ranch. It was dark and the town fairly quiet. It was that time of night when all of the stores and businesses were closed, except for the saloon, but windows were still lighted here and there. People were having dinner and spending time together before bed.

I sat and thought about Doc. I don't know if I would have begun wondering about him on my own, but now that the idea was there, I just couldn't shake it.

He was indeed a bundle of contradictions. When he helped Will Church and me face down that crowd the night he first rode into town, there hadn't been a shred of fear in his eye. When he wore a badge the day of the hanging and helped provide security around the gallows, again there was no fear or uncertainty. He held a rifle like he knew how to use it. He walked like a man who knew how to handle himself in any kind of fight. He wore his pistol hanging low and tied down, and it wasn't for show.

And yet, I had seen him set Billy's arm, and he did it with practiced hands. He set Billy's arm like he had done it more times than he could count. He delivered a baby in town a week and a half ago, and they say he handled it like child delivering was nothing new to him.

He spoke with an air of professional theater. Like many men of high education did. And yet, when you got him drunk, a hint of a Kentucky twang rose to the surface.

He had said one time that if I knew more about him, I would arrest him. I decided he was a good man and becoming a good friend, so I had chosen not follow up on that. But then I got to thinking, as I sat here and looked off at the town and drank my coffee, that maybe I should follow up on it after all.

I went inside and turned up the lamp. It was warm in here because of the stove, so I opened a couple of windows to try and get a cross breeze going. Then I sat at my desk and began going through the stack of reward posters on my desk.

Some of the names were familiar, some were not. I read the descriptions. None of them struck me as quite fitting that of Doc.

There was one man who was about his height and had the right hair color and was about the right age, and he was from Kentucky. But he had a knife scar that traveled down the side of his nose to his lip.

I saw a name I hadn't seen in a while. Victor Falcone. Another that I had heard of before, Kiowa Haynes. About as dangerous as they come. I remembered they both rode with Sam Patterson, or they had at one time.

None of the men in here could be Doc Benson. But then, Ike Hawkins had said Ambrose Conrad could change the way he looked. A master of disguise, apparently.

I decided to take a walk down to Doc's.

I found his office door locked and the place dark. He lived in a back room behind his office, so I rapped on the door a couple of times. No answer.

I then thought about it. Where would he be at this hour? It was a little after eight.

I headed over to Nell's. I found him at a table. All of the other tables were empty, and Nell was sitting with him. They were laughing and talking.

He looked up when I stepped in. "Tremain," he said.

Nell looked over. "I still have some coffee if you'd like some."

"Actually," I said, "I really need to talk with Doc for a minute."

She got to her feet and said with a smile, "I should be closing up, anyway."

She said to Doc, "It was great talking with you."

"If you would like," he said, "when you're through here I'll walk you home."

"I would like that very much."

She went to the kitchen and I sat down at the table.

Doc said, "What's on your mind?"

I had told him earlier about Ambrose Conrad. I said to him, "I've gotta ask you some questions. I hate to do this."

"So, you think I might be this man?"

I shrugged. I wanted to say that I didn't. My gut feeling was that he probably wasn't. But there was that nagging little doubt hanging in the back of my mind.

"Who are you, Doc? Who are you really? You seem to know your doctorin', but you wear a gun like you know how to use it. You know your way around high society folks, but you also seem to know how to handle yourself in a fight."

He gave me a long look. "I thought I knew you better than that."

I held one hand up as if to say *slow down*. "Maybe I'm being a little over cautious because of what happened last year. It's just that I know how dangerous Hooper was. We can't take any chances with his brother."

"Has it occurred to you that if I were this Avenging Angel, I would have already killed you by now?"

"Actually, you have a point there."

But Doc's back hairs were already up. "I thought when you gave me a badge, you trusted me."

"I do. It's just that you seem to be something of a mystery."

"Am I under arrest for anything?"

"No, Doc. No"

He dug into his vest pocket and dropped his tin star on the table. "Since you apparently don't trust me, I won't be needing this."

"Now, Doc, wait-a-minute."

Before I could say anything else, he said, "If I'm not under arrest for anything, could you please leave me alone so I could enjoy my coffee in peace?"

I pushed the chair back and got to my feet. He took his cup for a sip, but kept his gaze down at the table.

I turned away and headed back to my office.

I cursed this whole thing. It was causing me to doubt people I had no business doubting. Hooper had a way of getting under your skin, and apparently his brother did, too.

The following morning, I decided to go down and give Doc an apology. He had become a good friend. I know if our positions had been reversed, I might have become a little riled at being questioned, too. I might have experience at tracking a man and bringing him in, but when it came to the more subtle aspects of being a town lawman, I realized I still had a lot to learn.

I found Doc outside his office. He had a horse saddled as though he was about to mount up. He wasn't in his characteristic jacket and vest and tie, but instead a range shirt and jeans, and a worn-looking stetson that was sort of a desert-neutral color. A rifle was in his saddle boot.

Joe stood behind him on the boardwalk, his scattergun raised and ready for business. Jericho was beside him, his rifle held in both hands, not quite aimed at Doc but ready to be brought up to fire if necessary. Will Church was there, off to one side and flanking Doc. Will's revolver was in his hand.

I heard Joe said, "Step away from that there horse, Doc, and drop that gun."

Doc held the rein in one hand and he let it fall away, but he didn't step away from the horse. He let his right hand drop to within reaching distance of his gun.

He said, "I've never given up my gun, and I'm

not going to start now."

Joe said, "I got me a scatter gun trained on you. You know what that can do to a man."

"Depends on if you can fire it before I can clear leather."

I called out to both of them, "Now, hold on!"

Joe said, "Doc is fixin' to ride on out."

I said, "That true, Doc?"

"As if it's any of your business. I was planning on a ride through the hills outside of town."

Joe said, "You need a rifle for that?"

"Wouldn't you? With that Avenging Angel character out and about?"

I walked up to Doc to stand between him and Joe. I said to Joe, "Lower that shooting iron, Joe."

He did.

I said, "You gotta admit, Doc, after the conversation we had last night, it looks a little odd."

"Really?" he said. "What is it that you think I'm doing?"

Joe said, "You could be Ambrose Conrad. We're getting too close to figuring this out, so you're gettin' out of town while the gettin' is good."

"Maybe I'm just going for a ride to enjoy the morning air. Maybe I do that from time to time."

"Not that I've ever seen," I said. "You're such a man of precision. Breakfast at Nell's every morning. Coffee at my office around ten or eleven. I've never seen you saddle up and take a joy ride."

"You do seem to be aware of my habits."

"My job. A town marshal has to be able to know when something is off. I know Cyrus Henley opens the general store about seven every morning, and at seven-ten he's out front sweeping off the boardwalk. I know Nell fires up her stove every morning at six-thirty to have it ready to start serving breakfast at about the same time Cyrus is opening his store. If something in these morning routines is off, I notice."

Doc looked at me. "I consider you a friend. But I'm not surrendering my sidearm or my rifle to you or any man."

I said, "At least until we get this figured out." He shook his head.

It was clear Doc's ire was up. He was generally a calm man, but every man has his trigger. Maybe we had found his. Doubting his word, or telling him to drop his gun. Maybe both. I have to admit, in his place I would have felt the same.

And yet, I had a job to do. If we were wrong about Doc, we could apologize later. But on the off chance that he was this Ambrose Conrad, we had to make sure he didn't just ride away.

"Doc," I said. "If you've got nothing to hide, give me your gun."

I had never seen Doc angry or stubborn. Until now.

He said, "Take it from me. If you think you can."

24

I DIDN'T WANT to fight Doc. I sure didn't want Joe
or Jericho or Will to shoot him. And I didn't want my
men to get shot. Not that I was very concerned about
Joe—he was a McCabe, and I really doubted there
were many men who could draw and fire before Joe
could squeeze the trigger of his scatter gun. But as
good as Jericho was with his rifle, he was a kid with
no experience, and Will was a cowhand, not a
gunhand. Something about Doc told me he had more
than enough experience at this sort of thing.
Especially if he really was Ambrose Conrad. I'll take
experience over skill anytime.

I said, "Doc, I'm only going to ask you one
more time."

"Take it from me," he said. "Or let me ride
past. But tell these deputies of yours with their guns
aimed at my back that if they don't lower those guns,
there's going to be some shooting."

Enough was enough. It was time to end this
situation, and I was going to start by taking Doc's
gun. He wanted to do it the hard way, and I was
game. I swung a fist directly at his face.

My fist didn't connect, however. Doc was
expecting the move, and blocked my fist with his
forearm, and then grabbed my arm and used an old
wrestling trick and threw me over his shoulder and
onto my back in the dirt.

Joe said, "Make another move and I'll fill you
with buckshot."

I scrambled to my feet and held out my hands
for them to wait. I said, "Don't anybody shoot. He's

mine."

I didn't care at this point if he was Ambrose Conrad or not. No one was going to throw me in the dirt.

I squared off against him. Doc raised his fists in front of him like a trained boxer. I didn't. I had learned a lot of fighting from Apache scouts I rode with, and I would fight my way.

He snapped a jab out that caught me squarely on a cheekbone and opened a gash. I stepped back a bit, letting him think I was hurt worse than he thought, and he took the bait and stepped in and snapped another jab out.

I weaved to one side, away from the jab, and then stepped in and drove an elbow into his face. It was his turn to go down in the dirt.

He got to his feet. My elbow had caught the bridge of his nose and blood was trickling into his mustache, but he was smiling.

"All right, country boy," he said to me. "You're going to regret that."

He charged into me, and I into him. We stood toe-to-toe, driving fists into each other. I caught one in the ribs. He took one to the eye. I felt one bounce off of my cheekbone. I caught him in the stomach muscles. They were hard as rock, but I heard him huff a bit.

I then grabbed him to throw him over my shoulder, but I couldn't get a grip on him, grabbing his collar instead, and I felt part of his shirt rip away.

Still standing behind me, he wrapped one arm around my neck, and I stepped backward and snapped my head back into his face.

I turned to punch him, but he managed to dodge the punch, and grabbed me. He tried to roll me over his hip to drop me into the dirt again, but I grabbed hold of him by an arm and pulled him down with me. The rest of his shirt ripped away and I landed on my face and got a mouthful of dirt.

We both got only to our knees before he drove a right cross into my face. I countered with an uppercut into his jaw and I heard his teeth clack together

Fighting is an activity than can leave you winded very quickly. He and I were both sucking air through our open mouths while we traded fists. I caught one just above my brow. I drove one into his cheekbone.

We were getting weaker. My arms felt heavy and I could see his did, too. The only remnants of his shirt were his cuffs that were still buckled to his wrists. Somewhere along the line, one of my sleeves had come away from my shoulder, and the buttons down the front of my shirt had been ripped away.

I was bleeding from my mouth and nose and from a gash on my cheekbone, as well as one on my chin that I didn't remember getting. He had a gash on his cheekbone and the bridge of his nose. Blood was now trickling steadily from his nose and one eye was swollen shut.

I wound up falling back to sit in the dirt, trying to catch my breath. My fists felt like someone had taken a hammer to them. Doc was sitting in the dirt, too. His holster was empty—at least I had gotten his gun away from him. I saw it in the dirt a few feet away. My holster was empty, too.

I heard a voice from somewhere above. "If you two are done playing in the dirt, I have some things to tell you."

I looked up to see Ike Hawkins sitting in the saddle, looking down at us. He had a couple of rangers with him.

I said, with my chest heaving for air, "This man could be Ambrose Conrad."

Ike shook his head. "No he ain't. You got the wrong man."

I looked at Doc, beaten and bloody. Doc looked back and me and just shook his head, but didn't say anything.

Ike said, "Look at this man's back. There ain't a mark on it. We've got some new information that Ambrose Conrad got treated with a cat o'nine tails more than once at that Mexican prison. His back is decorated with scars."

Doc said, "Now don't you feel stupid?"

I said, "Ain't the first time."

25

IKE HAWKINS SAT down with Joe and me in my office, and we gave him a cup of coffee.

My face was bruised and swollen, but most of the bleeding had stopped. I changed my dusty, torn shirt for a fresh one, then poured myself a cup of coffee. I sat down in the wooden office chair behind my desk, but I did so gingerly. I had landed hard on my backside when Doc flipped me over his back.

Hawkins said, "I don't know if I've ever seen anyone more banged up than you look."

I said, "I have a feeling it's all gonna be hurting even worse, come morning."

Hawkins told us about how they had caught a group of Mexican border raiders burning and looting a ranch down near the Rio Grande. One of the raiders decided turned the tables on one of his friends.

The raider said, "I know something you might want to know. Do you know the name Ambrose Conrad?"

This got the attention of the Rangers who had caught them. The raider claimed a friend had ridden with Conrad at one time.

"He didn't want to talk," Hawkins told us over coffee at my office. "But we persuaded him."

Persuading him meant hanging him from his wrists from a barn timber and sinking their fists into him until he talked. There were rough men on the frontier, and sometimes rough methods had to be used.

I had the fleeting thought that it's amazing the uncivilized things some men do in the name of civilization.

Regardless, this man gave us what we needed. A physical description of Conrad.

"He's fairly bland," Hawkins said. "Which I guess you'd have to be if you can change your appearance easily. But one thing that's a stand-out characteristic is the cat o'nine tails scars on his back."

Later in the day, Doc and I sat at a table in the saloon.

He thought he might have some cracked ribs, and he had to talk Nell though wrapping a torn bed sheet around his rib cage.

He had replaced his shredded shirt with one of his white dress shirts.

I had a whiskey in front of me, and so did Doc. We were both on our third. The pain was starting to ebb away.

"Look, Doc," I said. "I don't know how to say this, except that I was wrong."

He nodded. "I suppose I could have handled it a little better, too."

"Tell me, though, how is it a city-feller like yourself, who knows all about hors d'oevres and such things, can fight like that?"

He smiled. "My secret."

"Fair enough." I grinned. "I do have one question, though. Why were you riding out of town?"

"It occurred to me that if a man was coming to town to try and shoot you, he may not come by conventional methods. In other words, he might try to sneak into town. I was going to ride a perimeter around the town and cut for sign."

"Not a bad idea," I said.

In fact, it was an idea that should have occurred to me. Maybe I was letting myself get too rattled by all of this. I had never met anyone man who could cause the damage Hooper did to this area. I suppose the thought that it was almost like he was striking back from the grave was more disturbing than I realized.

I dug into my vest pocket and pulled out Doc's badge and tossed it onto the table in front of him. "If we're both done acting like fools, I need all of the good men I can get if we're going to catch this Ambrose Conrad."

He picked up the badge and slipped it into his shirt pocket.

Joe came strolling in, along with Will and Jericho.

Joe said, "Look, Doc, I owe you an apology."

Doc gave him a long look, then with one foot he pushed a chair aside for Joe, and slid the whiskey bottle over to him. Joe sat and the barkeep brought over three more glasses.

Will and Jericho got chairs. Jericho laid his Winchester across the table.

Will said, "You two sure do look banged up."

"You know," Jericho said, "If we ain't all careful, we're gonna wind up doin' this Avengin' Angel's job for him."

26

IF I HAD to go to church, I would rather have gone and listened to Pastor Eb at the Baptist Church. He joined us for coffee at Nell's sometimes in the morning, and seemed rather down-to-Earth. For a preacher, that is. But Maddie's mother was Methodist, and so I found myself dragged to Sunday morning service there.

Generally I avoided church. I know Jesus said something about whenever two or more are gathered in his name, but I always felt closest to God when I was out riding among the hills or the mountains, with God's open sky above me.

I had met the new Methodist minister when he arrived in town, and I had spoken to him briefly. A man of about fifty. He had receding hair and he wore spectacles perched on the end of his nose. He had a scholarly way about him, and when he spoke I caught a trace of mid-Atlantic. Maryland, maybe. He walked with a cane. I didn't ask, but I had seen men wounded in battle, and something about the way he walked told me he had taken a bullet to the knee once. Maybe he had fought in the War, too.

He seemed like a quiet sort, which I found unusual for a preacher. Most men of the cloth I had met used words like an art form, but not this one. And when he gave a sermon, he just sort of spoke in a run-on, monotonous kind of way. I found that to sit in the audience and listen was a challenge in staying awake.

When it was done, he met us at the door as we filed out.

"Oh, Reverend," Amelia said, smiling and

gushing. "A most enlightening sermon."

"Why, thank you," he said.

He shook my hand. "Marshal."

"Reverend," I said. His name was Silas Black, but everyone seemed to call him *Reverend*.

I was going to compliment him on the sermon but I couldn't actually tell you what it was about, so I decided to just move along and let someone else shake his hand tell him how good he was.

Tables were set up in front of the church, and a social was due to start as soon as church was out. Folks from the Baptist church down the street were making their way down. The deacons from both churches had gotten together to plan this social.

"Pastor Eb," I said, shaking Eb's hand.

I poured a glass of punch for Maddie and one for myself. The smell of roasting beef was in the air, and people were talking and laughing. Children were chasing each other in and about through the crowd.

Maddie looked beautiful, and yet I couldn't keep my thoughts from drifting back to the fact that she was actually quite wealthy, and I owned next to nothing. A man wants to provide for his wife, but Maddie's net worth was many times mine. She probably had more money in the bank than I would ever earn in a lifetime. Once her old lady kicked the bucket—excuse me, *died*—then Maddie would be even richer. She would not only own the Shannon ranch, but a house in St. Louis that was apparently a huge mansion. I had never owned a home in my life. The closest I had come was the old family farmhouse back in Missouri, which had been burned to the ground during the war.

"You're quiet," Maddie said.

I shrugged it off. "Just thinking about Hooper's brother, that's all."

"Well, sometimes a man has to put his job aside and allow himself to enjoy the afternoon."

I couldn't help but smile.

Doc was there with Nell on his arm, even though he hadn't attended either church that morning. It had been a couple weeks since our scuffle, and our injuries were healing up. He was now able to laugh without his ribs hurting, and I could sit in the saddle without being reminded of where I had landed when he threw me in the dirt.

Jericho wandered from the Baptist church down to the gathering, his rifle in hand. He was a die-hard Baptist, and hit services every Sunday. He had very little money, so his version of Sunday-go-to-meeting clothes was to brush the dust from his pants and boots and to button the top button of his shirt.

"Jericho," I said. "Do you go everywhere with that rifle?"

"Well," he said, "I figured it might be a good idea to have it close to hand. At least until we catch Hooper's brother"

Doc and Nell had moseyed over. Doc said, "He has a good point, you know. A gathering like this would be a great place for someone to take a shot at you or Maddie. Say, from one of those windows."

I followed his gaze to a point across the street. The hotel stood tall and grand, with a line of second floor windows facing the church.

Maddie was with her mother, overlooking the refreshment table. I went over to her and said, "I have to step away for a few minutes. Marshal duties."

Amelia rolled her eyes. But Maddie touched my arm and said, "Be careful."

Joe saw Doc and Jericho and me gathering, and came on over. Joe had left his scatter gun at the office.

"Joe," I said. "I'd like you to sort of wander through the crowd. Watch for any sign of anything that doesn't seem right. Jericho, stay over by Maddie. Keep your eyes open."

"Yes sir," he said.

Doc wasn't wearing his gun.

I said, "Are you armed?"

He padded his jacket pocket. "I'm never without at least a pocket gun."

"Come on," I said. "Let's go check out those hotel rooms."

We crossed the street and stepped into the hotel lobby.

The manager was behind the counter looking bored. A portly, middle-aged man with bushy, gray side burns. I asked to see the hotel register and he flipped open a book and handed it to me. Two of the five rooms on the second floor were occupied.

"We need to see all five rooms," I said.

We followed him upstairs with our guns drawn. Only three rooms had windows facing the front street, so those are the ones we focused on. I took the key and opened the door, telling the manager to wait out in the hall.

Only one of these rooms was occupied, so we checked that room first. A traveling gun salesman. We found the room empty. The large trunk was on the floor. I found it locked. The bed had been slept in, and the covers were rumpled.

The window overlooked the street below. I could see Maddie and her mother talking with the Methodist minister, What's-his-name. Jericho was standing with them, rifle in one hand. He was looking about, watching the crowd.

"This would be a great spot to shoot from," I said.

"But he's obviously not here," Doc said. "If he's really Ambrose Conrad, then he's missing a good opportunity."

"The way Hawkins talks about him, I don't think that man misses many opportunities. I don't think this gun salesman is the man we're after."

We checked the other two rooms. Both were vacant. I half-expected to see signs that a sniper had set up shop in one of the rooms without the manager knowing it. But there was nothing to indicate that anyone had been in the room for days, except for maybe the maid.

We stood in the third room looking down at the crowd below.

Doc said, "You know, maybe we're going about this all wrong."

I nodded. The bruises I had gotten from Doc's punches told me that.

Doc said, "We're thinking about this from the frame of our own experiences."

"I suppose that's what anyone would do."

He nodded. His fingers were rubbing at his chin as he thought. "We were both in the War."

"Union cavalry. I was a captain toward the

end of it."

"And I was an officer in the infantry. For me, I wore gray, but the experience was the same. War for me often meant one of two things. Marching on the enemy with bayonets affixed, or shooting from behind cover. "

I looked down at the crowd below again. "Marching on the enemy was about the same for me, except we were on horseback. And we did a lot of scouting."

"We have to think not like former soldiers, but like Pinkertons. The man is a mercenary and an assassin. At least that's what your Texas Ranger friends found out from that bandito. But he might not use the tactics we would expect him to use, based on our experiences. Hawkins said he could change his appearance. Something of a master of disguise. Very few know what he actually looks like. I'm starting to wonder if hiding in a room like this and shooting at targets below is a tactic he would even use. After all, to do this would mean facing return fire. He would then have to try to escape. It would be mighty hard, with Joe and Jericho right down there. Even if he got one of them, the other would be coming after him. And if you and I were down there, his odds of a clean escape would be even less."

I looked at Doc. "You saying he strikes from hiding? And then disappears?"

Doc shrugged. "I'm starting to wonder. Think about Hooper. From all that you've said, he wasn't a man to strike directly. He wasn't a man of the gun. A man of action. The apple often doesn't fall far from the tree."

There was that comment again. The apple doesn't fall far from the tree. It made me think briefly of how different Maddie was from her mother.

Doc and I went back downstairs.

I said, "If it was you, who would you be targeting?"

"Anyone involved in the hanging. You. Garrett. After all, he placed the noose on Hooper's neck and pulled the lever. Maybe Pastor Eb, even though he didn't actually assist in the hanging. Maybe the deputies who were helping you. Me, Will, Joe and Jericho. And maybe even Maddie, because she was instrumental in his arrest."

I stopped at the edge of the crowd. Maddie and her mother had broken away from talking to the Methodist minister. Maddie saw Doc and me and came over. Jericho was with her, like I had asked him to be.

I said, "Is everyone accounted for? Everyone who was at the hanging?"

"Why?" Maddie said. "What do you think is going on?"

Jericho said, "I saw Joe just a few minutes ago. He was going through the crowd trying not to look suspicious. But you know Joe. He looks like a half-crazy mountain man. He would stand out anywhere."

I grinned.

Doc said, "How about Pastor Eb?"

Maddie said, "He's right over there. Talking to Mother."

"Poor man," I said.

I quickly explained to Maddie and Jericho the

line of thinking Doc and I had started on.

Jericho said, "You know what? I don't think I've seen Mister Garrett."

Joe stepped into view, and came on over. There were probably two hundred people gathered in front of the church, now, and a fiddle player and a man with a banjo were starting to offer up some hymns. Joe worked his way through the crowd.

I saw Will talking to a girl. The daughter of the man running the former Brimley ranch. Sam was standing over by the punch bowl, alone. It occurred to me Sam might be a target, too. He was at the lynching, not wearing a badge but available if help was needed.

"Joe," I said. "Have you seen Tyler Garrett?"

Joe thought for a moment. "No, I don't think I have."

I said, "Come on."

Tyler Garrett ran a grain and feed store near the livery. I started down the boardwalk. Maddie hiked her dress up a couple of inches so she wouldn't trip over it, and despite her tight shoes with wobbly looking heels, she kept up with me. Doc fell into place behind us, along with Joe and Jericho.

We found the front door to the grain store locked.

Doc said, "As probably many businesses are on a Sunday."

Tyler was a man of about sixty. He had a son and grandchildren off in Kansas. His wife had died a few years ago. He was essentially alone. No one to report him missing.

There's no reason he couldn't have taken a

walk somewhere. Or gone off visiting someone who wasn't attending the social. But I had a bad feeling about this—something in my gut.

Maddie looked at me. "So, what are we going to do?"

"If we're wrong," I said, "the town will have to pay Garrett for a new door."

I drew my pistol and shattered away the glass window on his door, then reached in and turned the lock and opened the door.

We found Tyler Garrett hanging from a timber at the center of his store. A rope was about his neck, and his hands were tied behind his back. A sheet of paper was tacked to the front of his jacket, with the words, "The First."

27

MADDIE GASPED and took a step backward.
Jericho just stood and stared.

Doc ran to Garrett and grabbed him by the
legs and lifted, to take the weight from his neck. I
knew the effort would be futile, because I could see
Garrett's neck was already broken.

There are two ways to hang a man. One is to
hoist him by the neck, and with the rope pulling tight,
his air is cut off and he suffocates. This is what
happens when a lynching party puts a man on the
back of a horse and then leads the horse out from
under him. The other way is to have him stand on
something like a trap door and then have it give way
under him, and his neck breaks when the rope gets
pulled to full extension. This was what happened
here. I could see a chair tipped over on the floor under
Garrett's feet. Garrett had been made to stand in the
chair with the rope around his neck and tied to the
timber overhead, and then the chair was kicked away.

With Doc holding him up, hoping there was
still some life to preserve, I climbed up on a ladder
and cut the rope loose.

While we were doing this, Joe slapped Jericho
on the arm and said, "Come on."

They searched the premises.

Doc and I set Garrett down on the floor, and
Doc put his ear to Garrett's chest.

Doc said, "He's dead. Probably has been for a
few hours."

Joe said, "There's no one here. The back door
was locked. But there is a window out back that's
unlocked. Someone could have clum through easy

enough."

Nothing can break up a social quite like word getting around that a local prominent man was found hanging by the neck. People began packing up and heading home.

"This is horrible," Amelia McAllister Shannon said. She told Maddie she wanted to go back to the ranch.

Maddie said to me, "I can stay, if you'd like."

"No. I appreciate it, but I'd feel better if I knew you were home safe."

She nodded and gave me a quick kiss, and I held her hand while she climbed up and into the buggy.

"I feel I should go with you," I said.

She shook her head. "Your place is here in town. You're not just the town marshal, you're a Texas Ranger. And you have a killer to catch."

I was so glad she understood. Our eyes met for a moment, and I found I loved this woman more than ever.

Will would be going along with them as one of Maddie's cowhands, but I asked Joe and Jericho ride along, too.

I said to the three men, "Search the entire house before Maddie steps inside. The entire house. Every bedroom. The root cellar. Everywhere. And the barn and the bunkhouse."

Joe had left his scattergun with his horse, and he now had it resting across the saddle horn.

He said to me, "We'll take care of her, Boss."

I looked to Jericho. "Be ready with that rifle. I

know you've never actually shot a man before, but—
"

He cut me off. "I kilt a man once. Back in
Missoura."

I hadn't known this. But now was not the time
to hear about it.

I said, "All right. But be careful."

Maddie said to me, "You be careful too, here
in town."

Doc was standing beside me. He had a rifle in
one hand and was resting the barrel up and across his
shoulder. Where the rifle had come from, I didn't
know. I hadn't seen him go off to get it. He was
wearing his pistol, too.

Doc said, "He'll be all right. I'll have his
back."

I watched as the procession rode off.

"Marshal!" A man called out to me.

Barney Jenkins was running up the street
toward me. He was a smallish man with a balding
head and an unusually shrill voice for a man. He wore
a white shirt with arm garters and a leather apron
strapped from his chest to his knees. He was the town
barber and the undertaker. Right now, it was the
second profession that I had engaged him in. We had
hauled the body of Garrett off to his funeral parlor a
couple of hours earlier.

"Barney, what is it?" I said.

The man was flushed, and he was breathing
hard from running all the way from his funeral parlor.

"There's something you need to see."

Doc and I followed him back to his parlor.

He had the body of Tyler Garrett stretched out

on a table in a back room. The shirt was open.

He said, "I was going to start the embalming process, and then I was going to dress him in his best Sunday duds. But look what I found."

Garrett's face was that extreme pale that dead folks get before the undertaker applies pancake makeup to them. His chest was white, also.

But at the center of his rib cage and just off to one side was a cut. A slit, maybe three inches long.

Doc said, "That's a knife wound."

He stepped forward and Barney moved back and out of his way.

Doc prodded about the wound a little.

"A fairly wide blade," he said. "Probably a long one, too. It was slipped in here, between his ribs. The killer knew just what he was doing."

Doc looked at me as a thought struck him. He said, "Garrett was already dead when that rope was put around his neck."

Doc looked at the neck. "See, here. The rope left its imprint on his neck, but there are no rope burns."

I nodded. "A corpse can't get a rope burn."

"Precisely. A corpse could theoretically get a friction burn, but it wouldn't look the same as it would on live tissue."

We thanked Barney and then stepped outside.

I said, "He killed Garrett, then staged the hanging to make a point."

"I wonder where he could have done it? There would have been a lot of blood from that wound, but there was none at his store. And the killer apparently cleaned the corpse up, then put a clean shirt on him."

"Tyler lived on the second floor of his shop. Let's go take a look."

We went back into the store. In a room out back was a rickety wooden stairway that led to the second floor. There was a small parlor, a bedroom, and a kitchen.

I stood in the parlor, in the center of the room, getting a feel for things. Beneath my feet was a faded green rug. A sofa was behind me, and end tables that had fancy scrollwork on them. The kind of thing a woman would want in her parlor. Probably furniture he had from back when his wife was still alive.

I looked down at the rug. No blood stains. The rug was old and faded in places, and I noticed near the sofa and the end tables the rug was indented.

"Look at this, Doc," I said, and knelt down for a closer look.

Doc stood behind me. "What've you found?"

"Might be nothing. But see these marks on the rug?"

"The kind of marks made from heavy furniture setting in place for a long time."

I nodded and rose back up to my feet. "The sofa and the end tables were all moved just a few inches."

"Sign of a struggle? Afterward, the killer put things back as close as he could remember them being."

"But it was dark when the killing happened. The lamp was probably turned down. He didn't want to turn the lamp up at an odd hour and draw attention. So he didn't see the marks on the rug."

Doc glanced quickly about the room. "But

there should be blood. A wound like that is going to bleed."

I said, "Maybe not. I've seen knife wounds that didn't bleed much until the blade was pulled out."

He nodded. "You're right. I've seen that, too."

"And if Garret was hauled out of here and the knife pulled out somewhere else, then that's where any blood would be."

"And if he was dead at the time the knife was pulled out, there wouldn't necessary be a lot of blood, anyway. Dead men don't bleed."

I started pacing. I think best when I'm pacing.

I said, "Presuming this was done last night, in the wee hours, he's not going to want to haul a body very far. Chances are it was never even hauled out of the building."

We went downstairs to the store. Garret kept an upended barrel behind the counter for trash, but it was empty. We then went outside, and to a barrel in the alley.

I reached in and pulled out a towel. It was smeared with blood.

Doc said, "Pay dirt."

28

COME MORNING, I CHECKED in on Doc to make sure he was still alive.

Doc said, "Come to make sure I'm not swinging from the ceiling of my office, hmm?"

Then he said, "Sorry about that. Gallows humor. Literally, I suppose."

"That's all right. I doubt you've had your first cup of coffee yet."

"Perfect excuse to head down and see Nell."

The morning was cool, but the sky overhead was clear and I knew it was going to be another hot one.

As we walked down the boardwalk toward Nell's, I was about to say we should also go make sure Pastor Eb was all right. But then we saw him ahead of us, walking toward Nell's. He had a man walking with him, using a cane.

"That's the Methodist minister with him," I said. "Reverend What's-his-name."

Doc nodded. "Silas Black."

"Well, I suppose if a Methodist minister and a Baptist can have morning coffee together, there's hope for the Republicans and Democrats."

Doc laughed.

We joined the two reverends at a table. Nell came out and flashed an extra smile at Doc.

I said, "Pastor Eb, you really should be more careful, walking about town, until we catch this man."

Eb said, "I'm a minister. Just like my friend Silas, here. Ministers cannot afford to remain holed up behind a locked door all day. We have our respective flocks to tend."

Breakfast was served. Nell made a great rib eye, and I liked an egg fried all the way through. Doc liked his sunny-side-up.

As I ate, I said, "I'd like to ride out to the ranch and make sure Maddie's all right. Even though she has Joe and Sam and Will with her, I'd just like to make sure."

Jericho had ridden back the night before, but Joe thought it might be best for himself to stay out at the ranch, just to have an extra gun available.

Doc said, "I'm sure Jericho can watch things while you're gone, and I'm right down the street if he needs anything."

Almost as if on cue, Jericho came running down the boardwalk and slid on his smooth boot soles through the doorway.

"Marshal," he said. "You got a guest."

I gave a curious look to Doc. "A guest?"

I pushed my chair back and got to my feet and with my coffee in hand, I went to the doorway and took a gander down the street. A black buggy was parked in front of the jail. Sitting in the seat was the Mexican man Amelia used as her butler.

"I've got to guess that's not Maddie in there waiting for me."

Jericho shook his head. "She sent me to fetch you. She called me *young man*. She said, 'Young man, would you be so kind as to go fetch the Marshal for me.'"

I looked back at Doc.

Doc said, "This is why they pay you the big money."

The big money. Twelve dollars a month, and board, and the town paid for my meals at Nell's. It suddenly struck me as not being nearly enough.

I went back to the table and refilled my cup from the pot I said, "Tell Nell I'll get her cup back to her."

I had two other cups of hers on my desk because I tended to wander around town with my morning coffee, but I would get them all back to her.

I nodded to the man waiting in the buggy. I said, "If you'd like, you can go down to the restaurant and get some coffee. Tell Nell I said it's on me."

He smiled but shook his head. In perfect English, he said, "Thanks, but if I'm not waiting for her, she'll have a conniption."

I stopped in my tracks. I had heard him speak back at the ranch, and he had done so in broken English and with a thick accent. Now, his English was perfect. He had a touch of some kind of accent, but I couldn't place it.

I said, "I don't mean to pry, but you seemed to learn English mighty fast."

He nodded with a grin. "I'm paid to be a Mexican, so I act like a Mexican. I'm actually from Brooklyn."

"New York?"

He nodded. "My father's Italian. I came west looking for work. Got myself hired in Saint Louis by Mrs. McAllister Shannon." He shrugged. "The pay's good, so what the hey?"

I didn't know what to think about that.

I went inside and found her sitting in the upright wooden chair in front of my desk.

She said, "You really should do something about these chairs. They're not very comfortable to sit in for long."

I said, "I'll take it up with the town council at our next budget meeting."

She nodded with approval. She had totally missed the sarcasm.

I decided I wasn't going to play the high-society game this morning. The death of Tyler Garrett was still weighing heavily on me, and the thought that a man was out there apparently intending to hang everyone involved with the hanging of his brother was hanging over me like a dark rain cloud. No pun intended.

I could have offered to prepare her some coffee. I didn't. I sat at my desk and set my cup beside the other two.

I said, "What can I do for you?"

"I have an offer for you."

I didn't know what to say to that, so I just said, "An offer?"

She reached into her purse and produced and envelope. "Mister Tremain, I'm not going to mince words with you."

"Please don't."

"I need you to leave. Madelyn needs you to leave too. She just doesn't know it, yet."

"And where am I to go?" I had been told sometimes that I can have a bad attitude, and impatience and annoyance often brought it to the surface. This was often expressed in sarcasm.

"Quite frankly, I don't care. Anywhere but here. But put a lot of miles behind you. California, or some such place."

The envelope was stuffed full with something. It looked like a small paper pillow. She set the envelope on the desk.

"I have enclosed a large sum of cash. Take it, and be gone. Don't come back. Don't contact my daughter again."

I said, "Were my table manners really that bad?"

She gave me a look that said she didn't appreciate my humor. "We both know you don't belong in her world. You belong in this one. Dirty, remote little towns on the edge of nowhere. Madelyn belongs in Saint Louis. She belongs going to balls and drinking tea in the morning and fine wine in the evening. She needs to marry a man of prominence. She'll have a son who might one day be a Senator. She doesn't belong out here on that old ranch, raising livestock with a bunch of men who refer to a steer as a *cow*."

"Well, calling her men *steer*boys just wouldn't sound quite right."

She still didn't appreciate my humor.

"Mister Tremain, I can fully understand what you see in my daughter. She's beautiful and wealthy. To marry her would elevate your social status a number of degrees."

"Would it matter to you if I never gave any thought to Maddie's wealth?" Which was true, until recently. "And I have absolutely no interest in social status?"

"Mister Tremain." She shook her head slowly and a little sadly. "Everyone has interest in wealth and social status."

She rose to her feet. I did, too.

She said, "Mister Tremain, quite simply put, you might be a good man for the type of people who live in a god-forsaken town like this. You arrested that dreadful Hooper man last summer. He killed my husband and Maddie's father, and now he's gone, thanks to you. But you're bad for my daughter. It's as simple as that. Put your pride aside, and you must see that."

She started for the door. "Take the money, Mister Tremain. It's a generous amount. Good day."

Without another word to me, or waiting for me to say anything like "good day," or even "get the hell out of my office," she was out the door.

I heard her say, "Julio, we're going back to the ranch."

And then I heard Julio the Italian snap the reins and say, "Giddyup," and they were gone.

INTERLUDE
MADDIE SHANNON

MADDIE CAME DOWN the stairs in jeans and a range shirt, with her hair tied back in a tail. Buckled about her hips was a gunbelt.

"Madelyn," her mother said. "Must you parade about the house dressed like this? It's bad enough that you insist on vacationing in this god-forsaken back country. But do you have to dress the part?"

Amelia sat in a leather upholstered chair with a cup of tea in one hand.

Maddie said, "Mother, I thought I made it clear. I'm not here vacationing. I'm here to run my ranch. And I thought you were here to visit the grave of Father."

Amelia nodded. "Yes, I came here for that. But I also came to make certain you didn't remain here too long."

Maddie felt a wave of exasperation rise up within her. She was reminded of Sam's words. *The Shannon Fire.* She turned from her mother and strode toward the desk. She wanted to glance at a couple of ledgers, and then she was heading out with Sam. Eight hundred head were grazing north of here, and since these were longhorns that could run like a horse, and the pastures here in the West had no fences, the herd could easily spread out over two or three square miles. There were men stationed at a line cabin—not the one she had shared with Austin but another one—and she felt it good for the owner of the ranch to make an occasional appearance. Reinforce the fact that this was a hands-on operation.

But her mother couldn't take the hint that Maddie didn't want to talk with her right now—the subject was almost always the same, and Maddie had long ago grown weary of it. Her mother rose to her feet and set the cup down on a silver tray, and followed Maddie to the desk.

"Madelyn, you don't belong here. You must face it. I have indulged this as long as I could, but you don't belong wearing men's trousers and riding along like a *cowboy*." She said the word with distaste.

Maddie said, "Where do I belong? In Paris or London with you, frolicking about and drinking champagne?"

"Well, yes."

Their discussion was ended by the crashing sound of running footfalls on the front porch. Sam came bursting in through the front door. "Maddie!"

"Sam?"

"Maddie," he said. "You gotta come quick. We got trouble."

Maddie and Sam found Will Church in front of the bunk house. Will had his gun drawn and pointed toward one of the men. Maddie remembered his name as Chad Johnson. Sam had hired him a few weeks ago.

Maddie said, "What's going on, Will?"

Will said to Chad, "You want to tell her, or do you want me to?"

Chad was a man of maybe thirty, with a thick mustache and sideburns. He kept the point of his chin shaved.

He said, "They're all insane, Miss Shannon. Plumb out of their minds."

A tall, thin boy by the name of Oak Sanders said, "It ain't true, Miss Shannon. I seen it myself. Whip scars on his back."

Will said, "Take off your shirt, Chad."

Chad said, "I ain't taking my shirt off for nobody."

Sam stepped forward. He placed a hand on Will's pistol and gently pushed it downward. Will let his pistol drop until the bore was pointing toward the grass.

Sam said, "Chad, why don't you just save everyone a lot of grief and take off your shirt?"

Chad shook his head. "I ain't gonna do that."

"Why?" Oak said. "You got somethin' to hide?"

Other men had gathered about. Maddie glanced at them, and said, "Where's Joe?"

"Gone to town," Sam said. "He wanted to check on Tremain and Doc. I said he could go ahead."

Will said, "Get that shirt off."

"Easy," Sam said. "We're all a little edgy."

The news of Tyler Garrett's death and the way it had happened was fresh in their minds. And word had traveled fast about Hooper's brother being recognizable by whip scars on his back.

Maddie said, "Maybe we should send for Austin."

"Don't need him," Oak said.

One of the men lunged at Chad. He grabbed Chad around the neck, trying to catch him in a headlock, but Chad shook it off and sunk a fist into the man's ribs. Another grabbed Chad from behind, wrapping his arms around Chad's chest. Chad snapped his head back into the man's nose, and the man backed away.

"Stop this!" Maddie called out, but they weren't listening.

Chad drew his gun, but Oak was in front of him and grabbing at his gun hand. The first man Chad had knocked down was back on his feet and drove a fist into Chad's cheekbone.

Oak got the gun away, and then one of the men grabbed Chad's shirt by the collar and pulled downward. Chad was wearing no vest, and the shirt tore down and away.

"There they are!" the man called out. "Whip marks."

"Hold on," Will said. "Miss Shannon's right. Let's go get the marshal."

When the men saw the whip marks, they went into a frenzy.

One cowhand had been in the corral fixing to saddle a horse, and he jumped the fence and came on over. And there was old Harley Bird, a former cowhand and now the wrangler, They both joined the fray.

Will tried to pull the men away from Chad, but he caught a fist squarely between the eyes and staggered back and fell to the grass. Sam ran to his side.

Chad was now on the ground, with men kicking at him. Maddie pulled her gun and fired into the air. They ignored her and grabbed him by the shoulders and pulled him to his feet.

"Let's string him up!" one man called out.

Another said, "We can hang him from the hay loft!"

Maddie stepped in front of the barn, but they bulled past her, dragging Chad along. One man gave her a shove and she went down, and the foot of another caught her in the ribs. She wasn't sure where her gun went, but it was no longer in her hand.

The barn had a winch attached to a timber, above the hay loft door. One of the men threw a rope up and over the timber. A loop was tied in the end of it, and was forced over Chad's head and pulled tight about his neck.

Chad was barely conscious. One eye was swollen shut and he was bleeding from his mouth.

"Hoist him up!" one man called.

Oak had hold of the rope and another man joined him, and they began to pull.

29

THIS WAS when Joe and I rode in. I had been riding out to the ranch to make sure Maddie was all right, and I had an envelope I intended to return to her mother. Joe had been riding toward town. We met on the way, and he decided to ride with me back to the ranch.

I saw Maddie and Will on the ground. Sam was hurrying to Maddie's side.

A crowd of men were in front of the barn, and they had a rope around the neck of the young cowhand Sam had hired a few weeks back.

I drew my revolver and fired into the air, which caught their attention.

I cocked my revolver again and aimed it directly at the men. I said, "Next one moves gets it between the eyes."

One of them, a man I knew only as Slim, said, "There's only two of you. There's six of us."

They were all packing iron. Sometimes being part of a group of men can give you courage, but Joe had his scattergun with him and hauled back both hammers and aimed it at them.

He said, "This here hogleg'll cut three of you in half. Which three is it gonna be?"

When Joe talked that way, you knew he wasn't fooling. He had a way of talking through tight lips, and he looked at these men with the intense eyes of a man who has killed and was willing to do so again. Not one of them went for their guns.

I was going to tell the men to cut Chad down, but I figured I might be pushing my luck. The idea was to get out of this without any gunplay. So what I did was to say, "Joe, cover me."

I swung out of the saddle, and then I slid my pistol back into its holster. I pulled a pocket knife out of my vest, and I walked through the men and opened the blade and cut the rope that was around Chad's neck.

Being a lawman is often a contradictory thing. I was finding this out the hard way. I so wanted to run to Maddie's side, to make sure she was all right. But because I was a lawman, my first duty had to be to protect the innocent, and preserve law-and-order.

My knife was not as sharp as it could be. I knew Joe carried a bowie knife you could shave with, but I had to saw through the rope with my blade. Then I led Chad back through the crowd toward my horse.

I turned to the men who had been ready to lynch Chad.

I said, "According to the Ranger Ike Hawkins, the man we're looking for has scars on his back created by a cat o'nine tails. Any of you men ever seen that?"

They shook their heads.

I said, "It creates lots of thin but deep scars all over the back. Just three lashes from one can create a whole bunch of scars running all over the back. The scars this man has were created by a bull whip."

Chad's mouth was swollen, and by the way he worked his mouth and jaw, I figured at least one tooth had been loosened. But he managed to say, "I fought for the Union. I was at Andersonville. That's where I got these scars."

Oak said, "Why didn't you say so?"

"No one give me the chance."

I said, "We should get this man into town. Have Doc take a look at him."

Joe said to the crowd, "Can I lower my scattergun without any of you trying to take a cowardly shot at us?"

The men nodded. They were looking sheepish. Some were looking down at their boots and others were just looking away.

While Joe helped Chad up onto my horse, I went to Maddie's side.

She was on her feet, now.

"I'm all right," she said.

I said, "I'd still like Doc to have a look at you."

She shook her head. "I said I'm all right."

I decided to let it go at that. Maddie was all woman, but she had a Texas toughness to her that was stronger than most men.

She said, "You get Chad into town. Let Doc make sure he's all right. I have some men to fire."

30

DOC SAID Chad had some broken ribs, and one tooth was completely lost. Doc thought Chad's jaw wasn't broken, but his nose was. Chad had a black eye that had swollen shut, but Doc had seen black eyes worse than this one and thought he would be all right.

Doc was telling us this at the saloon, as we all poured drinks from a bottle of bourbon. Maddie and Sam were there. They had ridden in from the ranch to check on Chad.

I said to Maddie, "Chad's mighty riled."

She said, "He has reason to be."

"He wants to sue you. Though, I'm not sure what kind of results he'll get out here."

Doc chuckled. "Civil court is a concept that probably hasn't made its way this far west, yet."

Maddie said, "I'm so amazed at how quickly things got out of hand."

I nodded. "It's the way of mob mentality."

"It's more than that. It's the law of the gun and the rope. It's the way things were out here for a long time. Even with me, last summer. I was more than willing to put a bullet in Jonathan Hooper for the crimes he had committed. I was more than willing to act as judge and jury."

I laid a hand on hers. "No one can blame you."

"It almost came between us, though."

Doc said, "I think Jericho said it right. If we're not careful, this whole thing is going to rip us apart, from the inside out. It'll make it easier for this

Ambrose Conrad to take us down."

I then remembered the envelope tucked into my vest pocket. It was thick enough that it created an uncomfortable bulge.

I said to Maddie, "I almost forgot. I rode out this morning with the idea of returning this to your mother."

I pulled out the envelope and dropped it on the table. She opened it and found it full of money. Paper dollars. She began counting them.

"Two thousand dollars?"

I shrugged. "I didn't know how much was in there. I haven't opened it. She came to town yesterday and offered it to me if I would ride out."

Sam said, "I ain't surprised."

Maddie shook her head. "This tears it. She's gone too far. She's going to be on the next stage back to Saint Louis if I have to hog-tie her and put her on that stage myself."

That was when I heard a scream. A shriek, really. It was very slight, like it had come from a long way off and had been mostly eaten up by distance.

I glanced from Maddie to Doc. "Did any of you hear that?"

Sam said, "Sounded like a scream, didn't it? Or did it?"

I got to my feet and headed to the doorway. Doc was right behind me.

I stepped outside. I heard the shriek again, but this time a little louder. One cowhand just loping along on his horse had tugged on the reins to stop the horse and was looking back over his shoulder in the direction the sound had come from.

Jericho came running. "Marshal! It's the pastor's house!"

Jericho turned back the way he had come, and Doc and I fell into place running behind him.

We came to the house. A small, single-floor building with a peaked roof. The house had actual clapboards, not just the upright planks of most buildings that were slapped together. The clapboards were whitewashed, and there was a small picket fence and an attempt at a flower garden. Such attempts were usually futile in the dry Texas dirt, and I thought this little batch of flowers was losing the battle.

We heard the sound again. Loud and clear this time, and it came from inside the house. I went to the door, drawing my pistol. I decided not to knock. Whoever was screaming had to be in a serious state of distress.

The front door was unlocked, so I went in. Doc and Jericho were right behind me. Maddie and Sam had followed from the saloon, Joe had been out walking the rounds and had come running. Soon all six of us were in the small entryway, our pistols drawn.

I called out, "This is the Marshal!"

We heard a sound from further back in the house. Kind of a sobbing, whimpering sound. We followed it through a small parlor and into the kitchen, which was at the back of the house.

The pastor's wife was standing there, bent over and with her hands covering her face. And in the center of the room Pastor Eb was hanging, with a noose around his neck.

Pinned to his shirt was a sheet of paper, and

written on it was, "The Second."

31

DOC TOOK Eb's wife down to his office. She was screaming and crying and sobbing, and trying to talk but the words were coming out as gibberish. Too much of a shock, Doc had said. He thought maybe some morphine might calm her down. He asked Maddie to go get Pastor Black, and I asked Jericho to go with her. I didn't want her going anywhere alone.

Barney Jenkins and a young man working for him came and got the body.

I said to Barney, "I want you to look for knife wounds. Anything that might have indicated if it was the hanging that killed him, or if he was dead already when he was strung up."

Joe had been out walking the rounds when he heard the scream, and I asked him to keep doing so. Make a presence. Let the folks in town know the law was out and about. There was no reason to panic.

"But be careful," I said. "It's very likely you and me and Doc are going to be his targets, too. And Jericho, because he was wearing a badge at the hanging. And possibly Maddie."

Joe said, in his tight-lipped way, "Let him try to take me. It'll be his biggest mistake. I'll end this whole thing right quick."

I placed a hand on his shoulder. I had to agree, a man would have to be insane to try and jump Joe. But I knew even he was only human. A knife or a bullet could kill any of us.

I said, "Just be careful, old friend."

I gave Sam a tin star. I said, "Here. You're deputized."

Sam said, "What're we gonna do?"

I said, "We're gonna have us a look around Eb's house."

Sam said, "What're we looking for?"

I said, "Clues."

"I don't know nothin' about clues. I ain't no Pinkerton."

"If you get beneath the surface of detective work, it's really no different than tracking an animal. Like cutting for sign. You're looking for things that don't belong. Like, even on hard, rocky ground where a track can't really be made, you can see a rock that might have been scraped by a hoof, or a small chunk of dirt that might have fallen from a horseshoe. Looking for clues is kind of like that. Looking for something that doesn't belong."

And so we set to looking.

"Don't seem to be any signs of a struggle," Sam said, as we looked about the kitchen.

There were four chairs at the kitchen table. Three were placed precisely under the table, but one was a little askew. I didn't think much of it at first glance, but then Sam said, "See this here chair? Why would it be a little off-center like this?"

I shrugged.

He said, "Look at this place. The sugar jar on the counter. The coffee pot on the stove, right in the center. Everything's got a way of real precision about it."

"A little bit obsessive."

He nodded. "I've known people like that. My own mother was. I would sometimes slide a chair out of place just to watch her get all riled about it."

He grinned at the memory. He said, "I think this chair was used on Pastor Eb. I think he was stood up on this chair, and then the chair was kicked away so his neck would break. Then the chair was put back, but the killer didn't notice how obsessive the pastor's wife is, and so just slid the chair back and got out of here."

"That's good work, Sam."

He smiled. "I might make a good Pinkerton, after all. Maybe I'll have to move to Chigaco and start wearin' a tie."

It wasn't long before Barney came in, looking for us.

"Marshal. Sam. I found what you was lookin' for. A knife wound, just like with Garrett."

I told Sam about the knife wound Doc and I had found. That Garrett had been killed in his living quarters, then the body was dragged down to the store and hanged there.

Sam said, "He done it for show. He's killin' them with a knife, because a man with a knife can kill quick and clean. The hangin' is just for show."

"That's what Doc and I figure."

I found the back door had scrape marks by the door jamb. The door lock was really just a metal latch. Many of the buildings in these frontier towns were thrown up hastily, by men who weren't necessarily skilled carpenters. Doors often didn't shut tight, and there were gaps and spaces under them or between the door and the jamb.

"Look at this," I said to Sam. "I'd be willing to bet he used a knife here, sliding it through and then working the latch back."

Sam nodded. "Came in through here. I wonder if this means he did the killin' here?"

We left the house and started back toward Doc's. I wanted to see if Pastor Eb's wife was up to talking. She obviously hadn't been home when the killing happened. I figured she had been away for a while, then went back home and found Eb hanging in the kitchen. But I wanted to know for sure. And I wanted to know how long she had been gone, and where she had been.

On the way, we found Joe on horseback, trotting along toward us.

He said, "We didn't find anything at all. No horses have left the livery since last night. I'm gonna go ride around outside of town and cut for sign. I told Jericho to sit outside the office with his rifle handy, where he could see anyone approaching long before they got there. That way no one'll be able to get the jump on him. He's settin' there with a cup of Nell's coffee."

I chuckled. "Before long, we're gonna have all her coffee cups down at the office."

Sam and I went into Doc's. Maddie was there, and Pastor What's-his-name.

Doc said, "Mrs. Crumby is resting in the next room."

He kept a second room with a bed, for patients who needed hospital care.

I said, "How long do you think it'll be before she can tell us what happened?"

Maddie gave me a worried look. "Maybe never."

The pastor was standing, leaning on his cane.

He said, "She seems to be in a deep state of shock. Poor woman."

Doc said, "I found rope burns on her wrists."

This had my full attention.

Doc said, "I think we were wrong to assume she had gone out and then came back to find her husband hanging."

Sam said, "What do you think happened?"

Doc said, "I think she was tied up and made to watch while he was killed."

PART FIVE
SHOWDOWN

32

IT'S impossible to hear that kind of news without feeling a chill run through you.

I said, "So, he's not using the same exact method with each victim."

Doc rubbed his goatee, something he did when he was thinking. "You have to put yourself in the place of the killer. Think like the killer."

Sam nodded. "If I was in his place, considering the whole town saw the killing, I might want my revenge by making people watch as I hanged the people responsible. Tyler Garret lived alone, but Pastor Eb had his wife."

I said, "Thinking like a Pinkerton."

Sam allowed a little grin. "Like I said, I should go to Chicago."

Pastor What's-His-Name said, "So, if this is truly the killer's motivation, to make loved-ones watch while he does his killing, then are we to assume he might have been in town when Jonathan Hooper was hanged?"

Now, that gave me something to think about. I said, "I hadn't considered that."

Maddie said, "I think we all assumed he came to town afterward, looking for revenge."

The pastor said, "Though, I suppose if he was in town, he would have tried to stop the hanging."

"Maybe not." I started pacing. Not that there was much room to pace, with all these people in Doc's office. "According to the Texas Rangers, this man is an assassin. Not that I've known many assassins, but the ones I have known tend to be snipers. Striking from a distance, or up close only in situations where they could make the kill and then get away. They weren't looking for a fight, they were just looking to get the job done."

"So," Maddie said, "with all the guns you had on hand, maybe he just thought if he tried to stop the hanging, he would get himself killed."

Doc said, "According to Hawkins, this man is something of a master of disguise."

The pastor gave a sigh of exasperation. He was hearing some of this for the first time.

He said, "Then it could literally be anyone in town."

"Well," I said, "we can rule some people out. Like the people in this room, for instance. Well, most of the people."

The pastor grinned. "True. You don't really know anything about me. And you'd be wise to keep everyone at arm's length until you can fully eliminate them as suspects."

Doc felt his patient would rest better if she got some quiet, so we took the discussion downstairs to Nell's. I actually felt like taking it to the saloon, but I didn't think the pastor would want a whiskey.

Nell poured us all coffee. She had just got done baking, and we each got a slice of apple pie.

You didn't see a lot of apple trees in this part of Texas.

She said, "I ordered some canned apples. They just came in on the last stage. The pie won't taste as good as if they were fresh."

Sam had just eaten a mouthful. "It tastes like a slice of heaven to me, just the same."

And so, we began bantering around theories, but it wasn't long before we were talking in circles. Doc had stayed in his office to look after his patient. I would have liked to have him here, because he seemed to have a good mind for detective work, but we had so few facts, it probably wouldn't have mattered.

What we could all agree on is that this Ambrose Conrad man was in town, disguised, and striking at members of the hanging party.

I said, "It's not like Eb even had a part of the hanging, really. He was just there to offer pastoral services."

Joe said, "You know something? We should warn the judge who presided over the case and delivered the sentence."

I nodded. I hadn't thought of that. "Good point."

I rode back to the ranch with Maddie and Sam. Joe came along, too. I wanted him to remain at the ranch and watch over her. Sam was a good man, and so was Will. But Joe was a gunfighter. He had ridden the so-called outlaw trail. No one else at the ranch had quite the experience he had.

This also gave me the opportunity to confront Amelia myself. I still had that bulging envelope in my vest pocket, and now was a good chance to get rid of it. The look of outrage on the old lady's face would be a good distraction from all that had been happening.

But Maddie had a better idea. She said, "That money could be looked at as mine. Or at least, a loan against my future inheritance. Why don't you use that as additional funding for your office? Paying more deputies, and such?"

I truly wanted to see the look of outrage on the old lady's face, but I had to admit, Maddie had a good idea.

So after Maddie was safely at the ranch, I rode back to town with the envelope still in my pocket.

33

AS I WAS riding along the trail heading back to town, I heard the sound of a bullet cutting through the air and just missing me, but I felt its wind on my face. Then I heard the gunshot.

I urged my horse into a gallop, and swung around and hung onto the side of the horse with only my leg slung over the saddle. A piece of trick riding I had seen an Apache do once.

There was a small, rocky ledge up ahead, and if I could get to it, then I would have some cover. But the ledge was a good thousand feet away, and the land was otherwise wide open.

Another bullet hit my horse, and it staggered a bit and I let go just as it lost its footing and went stumbling and slipping and then did a full somersault in the dirt and came to a sliding stop.

It was laying on its side. I ran to it, kneeling behind it to use it as cover. I had my pistol out, and I scanned the low grassy hills with my eyes. But nothing looked out of place. There was just grass, waving about in the wind.

The horse was breathing hard and raspy. A hole three inches around was in its chest, and blood was soaking its fur.

I rubbed the horse's nose. "Take it easy, boy. It's all right."

Someone out there had been trying to get me, but got my horse. It might be hard for someone who hasn't ridden to understand this, but something like a blending of the spirits seems to happen between a horse and its rider.

I was talking about this with Doc over a couple glasses of whiskey one night, and he nodded in agreement and said, "A symbiotic relationship."

I didn't quite know what that word meant, but I think I had the gist.

Another bullet was fired, and my horse was hit again, this time in the neck. Now the animal was dead. He would have died anyway from the first shot, but the second one killed him instantly.

I waited a moment, crouching down and then rising up for a quick peek over the carcass of my horse, then I ducked again.

A bullet came whizzing by, kicking up the dirt behind me. This told me the direction the shooter was shooting from. Also, there was a hesitation of maybe a second between the bullet passing me and the sound of the gunshot. This told me he was firing from around a thousand feet away. And he was probably using a long-distance gun like a Sharps Buffalo rifle, or one of the rifles snipers used during the War. A Whitworth or an Enfield. All guns like this I had seen were single-shot.

Not that you couldn't make a shot like that with a Winchester or a Spencer. I would bet Jericho could. But most snipers preferred the larger-caliber weapons.

I eyed the rocky outcropping. It was still over two hundred feet away. That distance could seem like a mile with bullets coming at you.

I decided on a plan of action. It was not a good plan, maybe, but when someone is shooting at you and you're ducking for cover behind the carcass of a dead horse, you don't get too critical.

I reached one arm up and pulled the Spencer from my saddle. A bullet landed in the carcass of the horse, as a response. It missed my arm by inches.

All right, I thought. I had a run ahead of me. I had to assume the shooter could see that rocky outcropping, and as soon as I started running, he would know I was heading toward it.

I had always been fairly fast on my feet, and considering that smooth-soled riding boots aren't the best for running in, I figured I could make those rocks in fifteen seconds.

I knew the time it would take to fire and reload a single-shot rifle, and then sight in on me again. The shooter would get one, maybe two shots at me.

I pulled my hat from my head, then stuck the barrel of my rifle into it, and lifted it into sight. The shooter responded with a shot that took my hat from my rifle and sent it flying.

I then pushed myself to my feet and took off sprinting toward the rocks. I ran hard, my rifle in one hand, and my tied-down holster shaking to and fro against my leg.

I counted the seconds as I ran. How long to reload, and draw a bead on a target. Or find a target through a scope.

Then I dropped to the ground, going feet-first, sliding down to a sitting position. A bullet flew past, overhead.

I then sprang to my feet and continued on.

I wasn't in the physical shape I had thought I was. I found myself huffing for air as the rocks grew nearer. But I didn't forget to count the seconds.

This time I didn't drop, as I figured the shooter might be expecting that, but did a full dive forward. I hit the ground in a full somersault, my rifle skittering away on the slippery grass. A bullet whizzed by behind me.

I took the extra half-second to grab my rifle, then scrambled to my feet and was running again.

A third shot was fired, but I went diving behind the rocks and the bullet ricocheted and sent a sliver of rock flying.

I decided to try a trick I had seen an Apache do once. The sniper's bullets hadn't missed be by much. I knew from battles I had been in during the War and gunfights since that you can't always tell from a distance if you have hit a man. The sniper wouldn't know for absolute certainty that all three of his shots had missed.

I lay still, and waited. While I was there, I thumbed a sixth cartridge into my pistol. Then I worked the action of my rifle to chamber a round.

A shot went off, zinging away against a rock. The sniper was trying to bait me into firing back, to determine if I was wounded. I remained still. After a minute or two, he fired again.

I was thirsty. This rocky outcropping provided a little shade, but even still, it was hot. Not as hot as it was back east, during the war. The humidity of those eastern states amazed me. When I was in the cavalry, riding through the woods of Virginia, I thought the humidity was going to kill us faster even than the Rebel bullets. Out here in Texas it was more of a dry heat, but dry heat can still be hot. I would surely have liked a drink of water, but my canteen was still on my saddle.

And so I waited. I closed my eyes and listened to the sounds around me. The wind, the constant Texas wind, was rushing against the rocks around me. An insect buzzed away in the grass out yonder.

Another shot went off, this time hitting some rocks on the other side of the outcropping.

I waited.

The sniper waited.

I watched as the shade gradually worked its way along the grass, moving a fraction of an inch at a time.

An hour passed. Dang, but I was thirsty.

I eventually heard a sound that I knew was a boot sole scuffing on gravel. I waited some more.

There was silence. Then another scuffing sound. The sniper working his way toward these rocks, and his boot had scuffed on some gravel.

I waited some more. I covered my pistol with my left hand to muffle the sound as much as possible, and slowly hauled back the hammer.

He then stepped into view. A man over thirty but not much. A wide-brimmed hat, a range shirt and vest. Riding boots. He had a pistol in his right hand, and in his left was a Sharps with a sight affixed to the top.

"Howdy," I said.

He managed to raise his pistol before I fired. My bullet caught him in the left shoulder and spun him clean around. He was still on his feet and raising his revolver to shoot back, but I fired again and caught him in the chest. He fell flat onto his back.

By the time I got to my feet and hurried over

to him, he was already dead.

I took a long look at him, trying to figure if I had seen him before. He didn't look familiar. I rifled through his pockets and found a pocket watch and some chewin' tobacco, but nothing that would identify him.

I figured it would be a long walk back to town, but I had no intention of walking. The sniper wouldn't have walked. Somewhere in the direction he had come from would be a horse.

I went back to my horse for a long pull of water from my canteen. I was watchful, though. The snipers I had known in the War always worked alone, but that didn't necessarily mean this one did. But there were no more shots fired at me.

I started up a long, low grassy hill to find the man's horse.

I made it back to town close to dark. I had replaced the sniper's saddle with my own, and the sniper was tied over the back of the horse, behind me.

Jericho and Doc came running.

"This one took some shots at me when I was riding back from the ranch," I said, swinging out of the saddle.

"Is that him?" Jericho said. "Is that the Avenging Angel?"

I shook my head. "I checked his back. Not a scar to be had."

Doc said, "He hired someone to take a shot at you. That goes against his way of doing business, doesn't it?"

"I figure this man was hired to shake us up a

little. Give us more to think about."

"Well, we have more to think about, anyway. Mrs. Crumby died this afternoon. Quietly, in her sleep."

"The one witness we have," I said. "The one person who could have identified him."

Doc nodded gravely. "And now she's gone."

34

DOC SAID he figured Mrs. Crumby died of shock. Maybe her heart failed or she had a stroke. The sight of watching her husband murdered was too much for her to handle.

I went back to the Crumby house to look around further, and Doc and Jericho came with me.

"What're we looking for?" Jericho said.

I said, "Anything that might be out of place. Anything he might have dropped that can give us some sort of clue as to who he is."

We searched the house. We searched outside. We checked nearby alleys. We rifled through empty barrels and old crates. We found nothing. We then went back to the house. A thought occurred to me and I wanted to check it out.

Jericho and Doc followed me back into the kitchen.

I said, "She must have been tied up right in here. It would have been too hard for the killer to haul the both of them from one place to another."

"How'd she get free?" Doc said.

"That's one question. Another one is where are the ropes she was tied up with?"

There were no ropes on the floor.

"How do you suppose she got free?" Jericho said. "Do you suppose she just laid here for hours, looking at her dead husband hanging? Working your way out of ropes that are tied tight enough to leave rope burns wouldn't be an easy thing."

I said, speaking as the ideas occurred to me, "She was cut free. The killer was right here in the house when she began screaming. He cut her loose and then let himself out the back door."

"But why?"

Doc said, "A diversion. While she was screaming and carrying on, he slipped away through the alleys."

I went back to my office. I needed time to think.

I sat at my desk, and took off my gunbelt and dropped it on the desktop. My desk wasn't a roll top, but one of those newfangled flat-topped desks. My gunbelt was dusty from the ride back to Maddie's and the adventures I had on the trail. Jericho sat on a corner of my desk, his Winchester in one hand. He carried the thing so naturally you would have thought it was part of him.

"Jericho," I said, "what would you do if you were the killer? If you were in town, using a different name and maybe even disguised. If you wanted to hang everyone involved in the hanging of Jonathan Hooper. What would be your next move?"

He shrugged. "Let me think about that for a minute."

"A lawman has to think like a criminal. Did your grandfather ever tell you that?"

He shook his head. "No sir. He never told me nothin' about it, really. I just admired the man and knew I wanted to follow in his footsteps."

"Well, think like a criminal for a minute. What would you do?"

He looked off into space, thinking. He said, "I think I'd look at the targets that are left. Miss

Shannon is out at the ranch, and she has Joe with her. I don't know much about Joe. I wonder if anyone does. But that man has a look in his eye and a way of handling himself. There's no way I would try to get Miss Shannon out at that ranch with him there. I'd have to wait it out, until a time when I could get her alone. Then there's you, here in town. And Doc and me. Trying to jump you could be done, but one mistake and it would be suicide. And the same with Doc. That man has gunfighter written all over him, almost as much as Joe does. I think the next target would be me."

"Why?"

"Because I'm young. Face it, I look like a farmer. I don't have the experience of the rest of you."

"Are you afraid?"

He shook his head with a smile. "No sir. Not in the slightest. He don't know me or what I'm capable of. I might be all arms and legs and fresh off the farm, but that don't mean I can't handle myself."

"Just don't go getting cocky. Any of us can slip and let our guard down for a moment. And a moment is about all it would take."

"Yes sir."

He waited a second or two, then said, "I think if I was him, I might take me a little break. Let us stew for a while in our own fear. Let us start getting jumpy, maybe suspecting the wrong people. Maybe suspecting each other, the way we did with Doc. It seems to me that something like this is a chess game. Or even better, it's like huntin'. You just have to be patient and wait out your game."

"He must have hired that man to go take a shot at me. Why do you think he would have done that?"

I thought I had the answer, but I wanted to bounce it off of Jericho and see what came of the rebound.

He said, "I think he did that just to keep us off balance. If he killed you, then our leader would be gone. Joe and Doc might be gunfighters, and Sam is a good man, but you're our leader. Cut the head off'a the snake. Not that I mean to call us a snake, but you know what I mean."

I grinned.

He said, "And if the man failed to get you, which is what happened, it just gives us more to think about. So I think I'd take a break from the killin' and let us stew in our own juices for a while."

I nodded. I started thinking I could use a cup of coffee, but glanced at the stove. The day was still hot and I didn't want to start a fire in the stove. I thought maybe a walk down to Nell's might be in order. I glanced at my desk and the four coffee mugs now standing on it. Maybe we would take those back to her.

But before I suggested it, I said to Jericho, "I want you to quit your job down at the saloon. I want to hire you full time. We don't need you pushing a broom or a mop. We need you with a badge pinned to your shirt and a rifle in your hand."

He knew how things worked with the town budget. He said, "I'm really honored, Marshal. But how would you pay me?"

I pulled the bulging envelope from my vest

pocket and opened it. I pulled a twenty dollar bill from it and handed it to Jericho.

I said, "Here's your first month's pay. Courtesy of Mrs. McAllister Shannon herself. You can bunk here at the jail with me, if you want. As long as you don't snore too loud."

He snatched up the twenty. "You got yourself a full-time deputy."

35

APPARENTLY AMBROSE CONRAD WAS
following Jericho's line of thinking, because there
were no more incidents. We braced for one, though.
We patrolled in pairs. Doc even joined us walking
morning and evening rounds. I issued a curfew,
wanting all stores closed by seven o'clock and
everyone in their homes with the doors locked. And
yet, there were no more hangings. It was like Conrad
had never even existed.

Nell said one morning, in regards to the
curfew, "You're killing my evening business, you
know."

"Well, maybe the McAllister Endowment can
reimburse you."

Doc looked at me with a smile.

I said, "That's what I'm calling it. The money
Maddie's mother gave me."

"So, there have been no repercussions from
that?"

"None yet. But I'm riding out in the morning
to check on things. I haven't heard from Maddie or
Sam for a couple of days. When I get there, I expect
to get an earful from her mother."

Jericho insisted on riding with me.

"I think I'm old enough not to need a
babysitter," he said.

"Hooper's brother hired a man to take a shot
at you once. He might again."

I reluctantly agreed.

Jericho and I reined up in front of the ranch

house. Sam was standing on the front porch with a cigar going.

"Getting some morning air?" I said.

He shook his head. "Just trying to avoid the house. I'll be glad when that woman goes back to St. Louis."

"Think that'll be anytime soon?"

"Doubt it. She said she ain't leavin' until Maddie decides to go with her."

Jericho and I swung out of our saddles. Jericho had his Winchester in hand. I left mine in the saddle.

Sam walked in with us and said, "How's the search goin' for Hooper's brother?"

"Not well," I said.

Maddie greeted me with a hug and a peck on the cheek. "We weren't expecting you today, but it's great to see you."

"Just thought I'd ride out and make sure everyone is all right." I glanced at Jericho. "Brought my babysitter along."

We sat down to coffee in the kitchen. Amelia was there, but she excused herself and sat in the parlor. She was working a small wooden needle about the size of a pencil and making a doily, or some such thing.

I told Maddie and Sam about the sniper.

"Do you know who it was?" Maddie said.

I shook my head. "He had no letter or anything on him with his name. He did have a rather ornate pocket watch, so I have that at my office. We'll ask around and see if anyone recognizes it. Barney's buried the body at boot hill, and if we don't find a name soon, we'll have to make a little headstone that just says *unknown*."

"Wouldn't be the first buried like that," Sam said.

I told them about Mrs. Crumby passing, which was hard for them to hear. Then we started talking about lighter fare, almost to clear our minds, and talk drifted to the wedding.

"I'd like to get married in October," Maddie said. "Mother wants us to wait until spring, for an April wedding, but I don't want to wait that long. She also wants the ceremony to be in St. Louis but I have told her it's going to be here."

I said, "I had hoped Pastor Eb would do the ceremony, but I guess it'll have to be that Pastor What's-His-Name."

"Black," Jericho said.

"Yeah. Him. I just hope he doesn't put the whole crowd to sleep."

Maddie laughed. "He's not that bad."

Sam looked at me and we both said, "Yes he is."

"You twoare incorrigible."

One of the men came in to get Maddie. One of the men Maddie hadn't fired because of the incident with Chad. A mare was about to foal, and Maddie and Sam went out to check on things.

While they were outside, Amelia drifted into the kitchen.

"You haven't given back my money," she said, "but I see you're still here. Apparently you're not a man of honor."

If a man had said that me, I would have laid

him out flat on the floor. I wondered if she knew that, and if so, she was not a woman of honor.

I said, "On behalf of the town, I wanted to thank you for setting up the McAllister Endowment. You're paying this man's salary."

Jericho said, "I want to thank you kindly."

Amelia said, "I do not find this amusing."

Jericho said nothing, and went back to his coffee.

"Mister Tremain," she said, "Mark my words. You are not marrying my daughter."

She left the kitchen.

I said to Jericho, "That sound like a threat to you?"

He said, "I'm glad I'm not in your shoes."

36

A WEEK WENT by with no hangings, and no one shooting at me from a distance. Folks balked at the curfew a couple of times and one man told me I was overstepping my authority. But other than that, the week passed with no incidents. And then a second week followed.

I sat at my desk and a disturbing thought occurred to me. Doc was sitting across from me.

"You look like you're in deep thought," he said.

"Something occurred to me, and it ain't good."

"Want to run it by me?"

I said, "What if it wasn't Hooper's brother who hired that man to shoot at me?"

"Who else would it have been?"

I looked at him. I hated to even say it. "Maddie's mother."

He looked at me for a moment. He said nothing.

I said, "Do you think it's possible? Or am I just letting my dislike for the woman affect my judgment?"

Doc paused for a few seconds, collecting his thoughts. "In my experience, people from her walk of life often follow a different set of ethics. Because of their money, they are insulated from the law, so they sometimes don't seem to learn right from wrong, the way the rest of the world does. The result is they often don't have any more morality than a man who would stick a knife in another man to steal his wallet.

The difference is people like Amelia hire their dirty work to be done for them. They don't have to get their hands dirty. They don't have to actually see the corpse or wash the blood from their hands. It gives them a sort of abstract distance. Makes the whole thing seem a little less real to them."

"So, you're saying you wouldn't be surprised if it had been her."

He nodded. "That is indeed what I'm saying."

This was the week the ranches paid their cowhands, and I expected Saturday night my curfew would be suspended, whether I approved or not. A Saturday night in a cow town had a life of its own and no one man could control it.

The cowhands rode in, some of them alone and some in pairs or small groups. They began drifting in during the late afternoon, and by the time the sun set, the town was loud with chattering and shouting and raucous laughter. Cowhands were milling about on boardwalks. Guns were fired into the air. A horse race was taking place down the middle of the main street. One man was standing on the boardwalk kissing one of the working girls from the saloon like they were about to start their honeymoon.

I sat at my office. Doc was there, and so was Jericho. Doc had taken off his tie, and the top button of his shirt was open. Jericho was in his usual homespun pants and suspenders. He had taken scissors to his wild-looking hair, but it didn't look a whole lot better.

Doc said, "Did you ever take part in this kind of Saturday night festivity?"

I nodded. "I worked a couple of different ranches in the years after the War. I can't say I remember those Saturday nights very well. I remember the headache the next day, though. That was before I learned the right way to drink whiskey, and the way to avoid a hang-over."

"You'll have to share that secret one day."

On a normal Saturday night after payday, I would have sat in my office and listened to the noise. If I heard screams or the sound of glass breaking, I would take a walk down and investigate. But since the murders, I was taking more of an active role. Once an hour, I would leave my office and walk down to the saloon and check on things.

Around nine o'clock, it was time to head down to the saloon again, and Jericho and Doc went with me. We walked along, and my mind was filled with thoughts. One being that any one of the cowhands we walked past on the street could be Ambrose Conrad. I recognized a couple of the men, but most were new faces. Cowhands tended to roam from one area to another, seldom staying in one place long.

I also thought about Amelia McAllister Shannon. I wondered if it could have been her money that paid the man who had taken shots at me, back on the trail. A suspicion I dared not share with Maddie. If I was wrong, then it could come between us. But if I was right, I wondered what it would do to Maddie if she was to learn her own mother was capable of financing a murder.

I also thought about Maddie and me, and our wedding. Once we were married, we couldn't live at the jail. I had a bunk there now and that was good enough for me, but it could never be a home. We would most likely live at the ranch. But I would be living in a place that was entirely furnished by my wife. Owned by my wife. I would become part-owner through marriage, but I wasn't sure how I felt about. A man wants to provide for his wife and family. I would be marrying into Maddie's money, into the success built by her father and Sam at the ranch, and the money she would one day inherit from her mother. I wasn't sure how the idea set with me.

I had no further time to think about it, as a cowhand came running from the saloon, the swinging doors slamming into the outside wall. He was followed by another.

He said, "Marshal, you'd better get in there."

The piano music had stopped, and a woman screamed.

"Sounds like our cue," Doc said.

I went in first. I didn't draw my gun, but I loosened it in my holster. Jericho was behind me, his rifle in his hands, and then came Doc.

Three cowhands from the Shannon Ranch were squaring off against three from the Brimley place. They were ready to draw. "Now hold on," I said to them.

But it was too late. Guns were drawn and fired. Two men went down. I drew my gun.

A small swarm of men and saloon women had formed in front of the bar, in an attempt to get out of the line of fire. One man threw a punch and then another did the same. Guns started being fired from men who were hiding behind overturned tables.

Things went wild. The brawl at the bar was suddenly all around us.

Jericho tried to bring his rifle up, but one man grabbed the barrel and then another punched him in the face, and he went down and the rifle came out of his hands.

Doc grabbed the man who had punched Jericho and tried to pull him away, but then another grabbed Doc from behind and a second drove a fist into his face.

I fired my gun into the ceiling, but it made no difference. Two men were swinging fists at each other, knocking over a chair in the process. Two others were wrestling at the bar. One had the other in a headlock.

A man tried to tackle me, but I side-stepped him and he fell away behind me, then a second man charged at me and I clubbed him in the face with the butt of my pistol.

Jericho managed to grab hold of his rifle again and swung it and whacked a man in the head with the end of the barrel.

There was a large boom from behind the bar, and all at once, the room went silent and all eyes turned in that direction. The bartender was holding an old double barrel ten gauge in his hands. He had fired one barrel into the ceiling.

He said, "I got another barrel loaded and ready to go if'n you don't stop this right now."

His name was Milt, and he wasn't short but was thin and with a narrow jaw and only a few wisps of hair remaining at the top of his head. He created a kind of smallish appearance generally, but with that scattergun in his hands, he was the biggest man in the room.

The fight was now gone from the men. The one who had the other in the headlock let go of him, and then straightened the man's shirt and said, "Come on. I'll buy you a beer."

Doc was on the floor wrestling with two men, but now the wrestling ended and they all go to their feet. A sleeve had been torn loose from Doc's jacket, and his hair was flying wild. He had a bruised cheekbone from the punch he had taken.

One of the men said, "Sorry about that, Doc."

The man I had clubbed with my pistol was down on one knee, holding one hand to his eye. "Sorry, Marshal. I guess we got carried away a little."

"Come on down to my office," Doc said, "and I'll have a look at that eye."

Two men were lying on the floor dead from the initial gunfight that had begun the brawl. Jericho and I rounded up the ones who we figured had started it. Three cowhands from Brimley's. I had never seen any of them before. We marched them down to my office and locked them into our single jail cell.

I dropped into the chair behind my desk. Jericho took a perch on the corner of my desk, and that was where he was when Doc came back from checking that cowhand's eye.

Doc had a look at where Jericho had been punched in the face. He had a bruise and a cut below one eye, but Doc thought he would live.

Jericho said, "Y'know, Marshal, we never seen any of them three before."

I said, "That's right."

"Has it occurred to you that one of 'em could have been that Ambrose Conrad feller?"

I had to admit, it hadn't. I had been too caught up in the moment.

I thought about the faces I had seen in the crowd. I realized I had seen the man who had been holding the other in a headlock, but only maybe a couple of times. In fact, the bartender himself had moved to town after the Hooper hanging. Any one of these men could be Ambrose Conrad.

Doc said, "You know what paranoia is?"

I gave a smile. "I've never been much on ten-dollar words."

Doc snorted a chuckle. "It means when you think everyone is against you."

I nodded. "I've known people like that."

Doc said, "It would be very easy for us to fall into that. To begin suspecting anyone we don't know for sure is not Conrad. But if we follow that route, we'll all go crazy."

Jericho said, "I think that punch loosened a tooth."

"Then don't chew on that side."

I said, "Hooper was great at getting into your mind. Making you overreact until you got tired of it and then underreacted. And that underreaction could get you killed."

Doc said, "I would say Hooper's brother subscribes to the same school of thought."

Jericho looked at Doc like Doc had just spoken Latin.

Doc said, "They both think alike."

Jericho looked at me. "Then, what're we

gonna do? We can't hold everyone as a suspect."

"No," I said. "What we have to do is be careful. Watch our backs. We need to listen to everyone when they talk. Just make mental notes. If something seems off, then we need to tell each other about it."

Jericho said, "When Gramps was telling us all about the lawman business, he talked about the posses he rode on and the outlaws he arrested. But all we can really do about this here Conrad feller is sit around and wait, and watch."

I nodded. "That's about it. Oftentimes, that's what being a lawman is. Waiting and watching."

37

ONE WEEK BLENDED into another. We watched. We waited. But there were no more incidents. At one point I began to wonder if Conrad had given up and left town, but then I got to thinking this might be what he wanted me to think.

One day, Maddie came riding into town. Sam was with her. Maddie reined up in front of my office and swung out of the saddle.

I had been out walking the rounds and was coming up behind her as she went to open the door.

She was in a range shirt and jeans, with her gunbelt buckled about her hips. A Boss of the Plains hat was pulled down over her temples.

"'Mornin," I said.

She glanced over her shoulder with a smile. "Sneakin' up behind me, Marshal?"

"Just appreciating the view."

"Why, Marshal. Are you being inappropriate?"

"Tryin' real hard to."

Sam took the horses down to the livery, and Maddie and I stepped inside and greeted each other real proper-like, with long, tight hugs and lots of deep kisses. When we decided we would get into trouble if we went any further—it wouldn't do for any of the townsfolk to walk in and catch us acting like we were already married—we headed down the street to Nell's for lunch.

While we were eating, Maddie said, "I was talking with Maude Harper the other day."

Maude and her husband Ernie were running

the old Brimley Ranch, these days.

Maddie said, "We thought, in light of all this Ambrose Conrad business, the town is on edge. Everyone in the outlying ranches are, too. Especially after what almost happened to Chad Johnson out at my own ranch. We need something to help everyone relax. We were thinking a barn dance. Since the Brimley place is closer to town than ours, Maude wants to host it."

Nell was coming over with a kettle of coffee to offer refills, which I was always willing to accept. She said, "A barn dance. I think that's a heavenly idea."

And so the plan for a barn dance began. Maddie was right about the town needing this, as a way of relaxing and letting off the tension that had been building since the murders.

Two days later, and the town was buzzing with it. It was the main topic of conversation at the saloon and the barber shop.

Except for Jericho. He had other thoughts on his mind.

He came into my office one morning and said, "Marshal, I need some of that money that Miss Shannon's mother gave you. What'd you call it? A dowage?"

"An endowment."

"Yeah. I need some of that."

Jericho poured himself a cup of coffee and sat across my desk from me.

I sat and waited. Finally, I said, "Well, don't keep me in suspense."

He said, "I was thinking about how that feller

got my rifle out of my hand during that scuffle at the saloon. A rifle's too long a gun to use in a situation like that. I need a shorter gun, but I'm not too good with a pistol."

He took a sip of coffee and tried to hide his grimace. I'll admit, I couldn't make coffee like Nell did.

He said, "Mister Fleisher, the gunsmith, he told me he could saw off a Winchester right at the forestock. It would mean I wouldn't have as many shots. Maybe eight at most. But it would be a short gun that I could use almost like a pistol but have better range. The thing is, I need some money from that envelope of cash."

I nodded. "That's not a bad idea. Okay. All right. How much do you need?"

Jericho said Mister Fleisher wanted thirty dollars to do the job. I thought that was reasonable.

Jericho said, "I also need a Winchester for him to work on."

"Well," I said. "I already gave you one."

"I need that for my long rifle. I'll keep that in my saddle and use the other one for closer range shootin'."

And so, Jericho got another Winchester.

It took Fleisher five days, and Jericho had himself a sawed-off rifle. Jericho took some leather and rawhide, and using a knife as an awl, he made himself a sheath for the rifle. He attached a strap to the sheath so he could wear the rifle slung over his back.

"There," he said. "Now I'm ready for whatever gets throwed at me."

We were standing outside my office, maybe fifty feet from the front wall.

I said, "But can you actually use that thing?"

Jericho pulled the sawed-off from the sheath and jacked a round into place faster than I can talk about it, and held the rifle hip-high and put a bullet in the wall. Then he began cranking on the rifle and shooting. In six seconds, he placed six bullets all within a hand's width of the first one.

I stood, looking at my wall while the cloud of gunsmoke drifted about us.

I said, "I guess I just got my answer."

38

THE DAY OF THE BARN DANCE WAS upon us. I rode out to the Shannon Ranch because Maddie and I had decided to ride to the dance together.

Maddie's mother was getting into a carriage as I rode up, and I said to Julio the Italian, "Buenos Dias."

He said it back, sounding as much like a Mexican as any I have ever heard. "Buenos Dias, Senor."

I tipped my hat to Amelia. "Mrs. Shannon."

She ignored me.

I said, "I wanted to thank you again for the endowment you gave to the town, and to my office in particular."

"Julio," she said, "let's be going. The air is growing thick around here."

Julio said, "Si, Senora."

As he said it, he tossed me a smirk. And then he snapped the leathers and the carriage was off.

I climbed the steps and took my hat off and knocked on the door. It was maybe thirty seconds before the door was flung open and Maddie was standing there in a green checkered dress with a white, lacy neckline. Not too low to look inappropriate, but enough to give a man thoughts.

Without a word, she wrapped her arms around my neck and pulled me in for a killer kiss. My arms were around her and I couldn't pull her close enough to me.

I said with a grin, "A little forward, aren't we, Miss Shannon?"

She returned the grin. "No one else is home. Sam has already left for the dance, and so has mother. I sent Joe ahead, too, because I knew you'd be here soon."

"So, do you suppose anyone would mind if we were late for the shindig?"

"Why, Marshal Tremain. It wouldn't be proper."

"Who ever said I was proper?"

I followed her into the house. She said, "I've got to finish fixing my hair. Then we can go."

She started toward the stairway that led to the second floor, then turned and said, "Oh, for goodness sake. We can be a little late."

And she was at me with another kiss.

When we got to the Brimley place, the dance was in full procession. A guitar player was strumming away, a banjo was being plucked by a man who knew his business, and a man was sawing away on a fiddle. A man whose voice I recognized as Tom Brantley was calling a square dance. Tom ran the livery in town.

I saw Jericho milling about, a cup of punch in one hand. I was struck by how much he had changed in the few months I had known him. He wore no hat, as he seldom seemed to. He had gone to the barber with some of the pay I was now able to give him, and his formerly unruly hair was now neatly cut. He was now in a white boiled shirt and his suspenders were hidden under a vest. His tin star was pinned to the vest. His linsey-woolsey pants that were a little too short were now gone, and in their place was a pair of jeans. Joe had been teaching him to ride, and he now had black boots on his feet.

He still wore no pistol. As far as I knew, he didn't own one. But strapped across his back in his buckskin sheath was his sawed-off Winchester. I suppose with that in his hands, he really didn't need a pistol.

He glanced over at us and threw us a wave, and I threw one back.

I glanced about and saw Joe. He was wearing a pistol at his left side and looked like he might have washed his shirt, and had fastened the top button and was wearing a string tie. He was talking with Meg Harmon, a widow-woman of maybe forty who ran a boarding house.

Amelia was seated in a straight-back chair by the barn door, sitting alone but with her back erect and her nose in the air, trying to look stately and dignified and like she held herself above all of this.

"Come on," Maddie said. "Let's say hello to Mother."

I wanted to say something like, "Do we have to?" But I had to remind myself that she was Maddie's mother, and like it or not, your mother is your mother. So I tagged along.

Amelia glanced at us. "Madelyn. Marshal."

I tipped my hat to her. "Miz Shannon."

Maddie said, "Mother, are you having a good time?"

Amelia rolled her eyes. "Do you really expect me to? In a place like this?"

Maddie said to me. "I should stay and talk with Mother for a while."

"You do that. I'm going to mill about. Make sure everything is all right."

Maddie knew what I meant. Even though there hadn't been any more incidents in weeks, it would be foolish to assume Ambrose Conrad was gone.

She mouthed the words, *Be careful*.

I nodded and took her hand and she grasped it, almost like a mini-hug shared between the two of us, and then I left her to her mother.

Will Church was here, standing with Sam Wilson and some of the cowhands from Maddie's ranch. A makeshift bar had been set up with two pine planks laid across a couple of crates, and Milt from the saloon had a set up a keg and was serving beer.

"Marshal," Will said.

Sam nodded. "Tremain. Everything all right?"

Conrad was on Sam's mind, too.

"Seems to be. Won't hurt to take a wander around, though. Doesn't hurt for folks to see the badge. Might make 'em feel a little more at ease."

Glen Giroux, a tinsmith who had moved to town a few months back, was further down the bar. He had thick, dark hair he kept cut short and a bowler perched atop his head, and he was tipping a beer and chugging while he was cheered on by a couple of cowhands.

Sam said, "If old Glen gets any more at ease, we'll find him passed out over in a corner somewheres."

I continued on. Sam and Will decided to come with me, each with a mug of beer in hand.

We passed folks, tipping our hats and offering

a *howdy*.

"This here dance is a great idea," Will said. "After everything that's happened lately."

Maude Harper came by with a plate of small cakes she had made. We each had one.

Sam took a bite and said, "Mighty tasty, ma'am."

The Brimley Ranch was now owned by some corporation back east, and they had hired the Harpers. Ernie was an old cattleman. He was standing off by the barn, a cup of punch in hand, and an old Boss of the Plains hat pulled down over his temples. He was laughing with a bunch of men from town. One of them a tall, thin man by the name of Harvey who was the barber.

I knew little of Maude and Ernie. They were both gray-haired, and he had worked as a ramrod in Arizona before taking the job here. She had mentioned once that she had been a nurse during the late War Betwixt the States, and that was where she had met Ernie. He had been hauled in to a field hospital with a musket ball in one arm. I was also learning, at the very moment, that she knew how to bake.

As I was thinking about this, I saw Nell Hanson standing off at the edge of the crowd. It was then that I realized I hadn't seen Doc Benson here.

I said to Sam, "You boys seen Doc?"

Sam shook his head thoughtfully. "No, I ain't, now that you mention it."

He was probably off getting Nell some punch. I knew he planned to spend as much time with her as possible today.

We wandered over and tipped our hats to her.

"Pardon my askin'," I said, "but have you seen Doc?"

She shook her head. "He said he was going to meet me here. Billy somehow managed to get his foot stepped on by a horse in town, so Doc was going to tend to him and then was going to come right out."

I had a sudden bad feeling about all of this.

"I'm sure he's all right," I said. "If he doesn't show up soon, I'll ride into town and make sure."

She gave a thankful smile. "Thank you, Marshal."

Sam, Will and I moved along. When we were out of listening distance, we stopped and Sam said, "You think everything's all right?"

"I'm not sure." I looked to Will. "Go get Jericho. Be discreet about it."

He nodded and headed off.

I looked over at the makeshift bar, and saw Joe was watching me. I gave him a little beckoning motion with my head, and he started over.

He said, "We got trouble?"

I said, "I hope not."

I saw Jericho and Will working their way through the crowd toward us.

I said, "Doc's missing. Nell said he was treating Billy in town."

Joe nodded his head. "I heard the fool boy got his foot stepped on by a horse. That was a couple hours ago. Doc should be here by now."

"Might be nothing," I said.

Joe looked me in the eye. "But your gut says otherwise."

I said, "You got your scattergun?"

His turn to nod. "In my saddle."

"Go fetch it, then. We'll wait right here. But be casual about it. I don't want to frighten anyone here in the crowd. If Conrad is here, he could be watching us right now. If everyone gets scared and starts taking off, we could lose him in the crowd."

Joe nodded and started through the crowd, toward his horse.

I said to the others, "Let's go over and have a beer while we wait for Joe. Everything's all right. We're just a bunch of friends enjoying a Saturday afternoon barn dance. Don't touch your guns or check your loads or anything."

We strolled over to the makeshift bar.

"Milt," I said.

"Marshal."

"I was gonna have some of that punch, but then I decided a mug of beer had a better sound to it."

He grinned. "Comin' right up."

I set a nickel on the bar. He scooped up the nickel and set a foaming mug in its place.

Maude Harper came by, her tray empty.

"Ma'am," Jericho said, "you ain't got any more of them cakes, by any chance?"

"Why, I sure do, young man. I'm heading back to the kitchen for some more right now."

A thought occurred to me. One of those gut feelings, again.

"Maude," I said. "Before you do, could you do me a favor?"

"Why, sure, Marshal."

"Could you go and fetch Ernie for me? I have

somethin' I have to talk over with him."

"Why, sure thing, marshal. I'll be right back."

Sam Wilson said, "You think Ernie Harper's involved in any of this somehow?"

I shook my head. "I just don't want anyone going back to any of the buildings until we've had a chance to search them. Just in case."

He nodded.

I figured Joe would be back before Maude could fetch Ernie. I was right. When Ernie got to talking, it was hard to pull him away.

"All right," I said, setting down the mug. "Let's just stroll our way toward the main house. Real casual-like. We'll start there. I want all the buildings searched."

Jericho said, "Shouldn't we go into town? Seems to me if Doc's in trouble, it would be there."

I shook my head. "Last time, Conrad hanged Tyler Garrett practically under everyone's nose."

Joe said, "If he was gonna do somethin' to Doc, it would be right out here."

I said, "Let's go check the house."

We got to the kitchen door. It was then that I drew my revolver and quickly checked the loads. I heard a leathery sliding sound behind me, and knew Jericho had pulled his sawed-off.

"Jericho," I said. "Will. Sam. I want you three to go around to the front door and start in. Joe and I'll go in through the kitchen. We'll meet you somewhere in the middle. We'll give you a count of thirty before we go in."

Joe and I stood and watched the other three hurry around to the front of the house.

I was counting to myself, and when I reached thirty, I said, "Let's go."

I opened the door and stepped in. Joe was right behind me. I heard the front door open and the scuffle of boots on the wooden floor. Sam and the others were in.

I glanced about the kitchen. It was warm in here because Mrs. Harper had been baking, and a wood stove can heat up a kitchen something fierce. The smell of those cakes of hers was in the air, and I'll admit it was a mighty good smell.

Nothing looked amiss. At least at first glance.

I nodded with my heard toward a doorway that would lead to the dining room. Joe followed.

We heard Sam call out. "Tremain!"

With my pistol held up for a quick shot, I ran through the dining room, Joe's feet landing hard behind me.

We burst from the dining room into a parlor, and that was when we saw it.

Doc was there. A rope around his neck. He was hanging from the ceiling.

39

I STOOD AND stared. *No, not Doc.*

"Cut him down," I said.

The rope around his neck was tied like a hangman's noose. A hole had been punched through the plaster ceiling, and the rope was apparently tied onto a timber. Doc's hands were bound behind him. Pinned to the front of his shirt was a sheet of paper that read, *The Third.*

"Cut him down," I said.

Jericho slid his rifle back into the sheath on his back, then pulled out a pocket knife and opened it up. He and Will pulled over a coffee table, and Jericho climbed up and began sawing away on the rope.

Sam and I grabbed hold of Doc's legs and held him so he wouldn't crash onto the floor.

Doc wasn't in his usual three-piece suit. He had been going casual today. At least, casual for him. He had on a white boiled shirt and a tan corduroy jacket, and a string tie. There was a blood stain growing on the front of his shirt. Like the others, I figured, he had been stabbed first and then hung by the neck for effect.

We lowered the body onto the floor. While we were doing this, Will Church stood with his gun in his hand, looking from the doorway to the kitchen, to the doorway leading out to the entryway.

I said, "Good thinking, Will. There's no reason to believe he's not still in the house somewheres."

"We should search it," Jericho said.

I nodded. "You do that. You and Will."

From what I remembered from being in this house before, especially the summer before when Jonathan Hooper had used the place as his residence, there was another corridor off at the other side of the entryway which led down to the library he had used as his office. On the second floor were bedrooms.

Jericho looked at me. "What if we find someone?"

Will said, "If this Conrad feller is so good at disguises, how will we know it's him?"

I was so angry my hands were shaking a little. I said, "Anyone who doesn't look like he belongs in here, shoot him."

I saw a look in Jericho's eyes I had never seen before. Sort of a steely mixture of sadness and anger.

He said, "We can do that."

And he and Will were off.

I knelt down by Doc's body. He had been a man of mystery, but one of the most capable I had ever met. I couldn't imagine who could possibly have gotten the jump on him.

I shook my head and said, "Aw, Doc."

That was when Doc sucked in some air, and coughed.

"He's alive," Sam said.

Doc coughed again, and then inhaled and then let the air out. He was definitely breathing.

"Doc?" I said.

He stirred a bit. Moved his head a little.

I tore open his shirt for a look at the wound. To my surprise, it didn't look like it had been done with a knife. It looked more like a gunshot wound.

I said, "Sam. Go get Maude Harper. She worked as a nurse back during the war. But do it easy. Don't act alarmed."

After Sam left, I said to Joe, "We've gotta stop this bleeding."

"How can a man survive a hangin'?" He pulled a bandana from his vest pocket while he spoke.

I pressed the bandana against the wound. I said, "I knew a man years ago was hanged, but lived through it. He said as long as they don't break your neck when they string you up, you can tighten your neck muscles and actually hold on for a while. But you'll eventually suffocate. It's hard to breathe with a rope around your neck."

"He must have been awake, apparently. At least when he was strung up."

Doc said, in a very hoarse voice, "I'm awake now."

"Doc," I said. "What happened? Did you see who it was?"

He nodded, and by the way he grimaced I figured the motion was painful. He said, "That minister. What's-his-name."

"Silas Black?"

He grinned. "That's the one."

I couldn't help but grin back. Even now, Doc had the presence of mind to make a joke and reverse it on me.

"I've got this," Joe said. "Go get him."

I stepped outside and gave a quick look around. If Silas Black was within shooting distance, I intended to put a bullet in him. I would worry about what a judge would say later. But all I saw was the edge of the crowd, maybe a couple hundred feet away. And I saw Sam hurrying toward the house with Maude and Ernie.

I said to them, "He's awake. I don't know how long he was hanging there."

"Couldn't be long," Maude said. "I was just in there half an hour ago."

"Looks like he took a bullet to the ribs, too."

"God bless him," she said, and ran into the house.

I said to Sam, "Go get Jericho and Will, then you all come and find me. It's Silas Black. He's the one."

"The minister?"

I nodded.

I had to think quickly. If my gun was out, people would know something was wrong. And if Conrad was in the crowd and knew that I was on to him, he might start shooting. In a crowd this size, people could get hurt.

I loaded in a sixth cartridge, then slid my gun back into its holster. But I didn't push it in too tight. I wanted it loose, so I could grab it quickly.

I then began to work through the crowd. Nodding to one person, then greeting another. "Howdy Ted. Willy. Good to see you, Helen."

I stopped at the bar. Milt said, "Marshal. You didn't finish your beer."

"No," I said. "I got pulled away. Say," I was trying to sound casual. Not urgent at all. "Have you seen Pastor Black?"

He thought a moment, and shook his head. "No I ain't. But I suppose I wouldn't expect to see a minister here at the bar."

I grinned. "I suppose not. Thanks, Milt."

I continued to work my way through the crowd. The entire town was here, in the Brimley front yard. This ranch yard wasn't small, but when you have a few hundred people here, there wasn't a whole lot of space left over.

If I couldn't find him here, then the men and I were going to have to search the outbuildings. There was a bunkhouse as well as the barn. And that little tool shed Maddie and Joe and I had been locked in, when we got ourselves captured by Hooper last summer.

I thought of the barn. There was a hayloft that overlooked a good section of the front yard. You could get off a good rifle shot from that loft.

I turned to look at it, and saw the loft doors were shut tight. There was no window up there. No one was going to get off a shot unless they opened those doors.

I saw Amelia, still sitting at the gazebo. I walked on over.

It occurred to me I should tell Maddie what was going on. Maybe she could go in and help Maude.

"Ma'am," I said.

"Don't you *ma'am* me, you highway robber."

I couldn't help but grin. "You're referring to your generous endowment to the town."

"I would appreciate if you stop calling it that."

"I suppose I could call it pay-off money. But that's not a very respectable thing for someone in high society to do, now, is it?"

She just glared at me.

I said, "Have you seen Maddie?"

She nodded. "Yes. She left a little while ago."

I blinked. "She left?"

"Yes. She was needed in town. She left with that nice minister. The Reverend Silas Black."

40

IT WAS then that Joe found me. Jericho, Sam and Will were right behind him.

Joe said, "Maude told us to go send Nell in to help. She knows what she's doin', though. Has Ernie tearin' up bedhsheets to use as a bandage."

I said, "He's got Maddie."

Amelia was on her feet. "Is there a problem? They left for town maybe fifteen minutes ago."

I looked from Joe to Sam. "While we were in the house."

Sam shook his head. "He knows what he's doing. That's for sure."

We had left our horses saddled, just with the girths loosened. We tightened them and mounted up and were off to town.

Joe said, "Has it occurred to you that we'll be riding into a trap? He has to know we're coming for him."

"Makes sense," I said as we rode. We were keeping our horses to a canter. I had to speak up over the hooves pounding into the dirt. "It's what I would do."

"Think like a criminal," Jericho said.

"That's how it's done."

Joe said, "He usually strikes one person at a time. He's after one of us. He's usin' Maddie as bait. When he's done, he'll kill her, too."

I said to Joe, "If you were in his place, which one of us would you be targeting right now?"

Without hesitation, he said, "You."

I was riding with Joe to one side of me and Sam to the other. Jericho and Will were right behind us.

Jericho said, "You're our leader. He might figure with you out of the way, he has a better chance at getting the rest of us. Like I said before. Cut the head off'n a snake."

The Brimley ranch was about two miles from town. When we had maybe a quarter mile to go, we reined up.

I said, "We ride down the main street, he's going to be waiting for us. He'll be able to pick off any one of us. And maybe even two, if he's a good enough shot."

"So, what do you recommend?" Sam said.

"We're going in on foot. We'll go in from the north side. Cut in through an alley."

Will said, "In all that whole town, how can we possibly know where he would be?"

Joe said to me, "Where would you be?"

"I'd take to the high ground," I said, and Joe nodded. I said, "I'd want a clean view of the main street. And I'd keep Maddie with me. I would be using her not only as bait, but as a shield."

Will said, "You think maybe he's on a roof top?"

Sam shook his head. "It'd be too hot up there."

"The livery stable," Jericho said.

I nodded. I was thinking about the idea of shooting from a hay loft, again.

I said, "From the loft, he would have a clear field of fire up and down the street. Anyone gets within a couple of blocks, and they could be taken out with a rifle."

Sam said, "He'd have to be an awful good shot."

"I don't think we should underestimate him at all."

"Smart thinkin'," Joe said. "That's what my brother would say."

"Who's your brother?" Jericho said.

"Someone you don't need to worry about."

I said, "That livery barn is gonna be hard to approach. There's one door to the back, but that can be barred from the inside. He'll hear it if we should break a window to get in."

Joe said, "The only way to approach it will be from the front."

I nodded. "He'll be in the hay loft. He'll be there, watching for us."

Sam said, "He's gonna have to have a way to escape afterward. I don't see how he could. Even if he plugs two of us, he can't shoot us all."

"The way he's been doing things so far is to create distractions," Joe said. "I've gotta think that's what he'll do now, too."

I looked at him. "What kind of distraction would you create?"

Joe shrugged. "Fire, maybe. He's right there in the livery barn. All that hay. I would have a whole bunch of it already soaked with kerosene. He shoots one of us from the loft, then throws a match and runs."

"And Maddie'll be right there in the fire."

"I hate to say this," Sam said, "but if we got

about this like we're afraid he's gonna hurt her, then he's got a powerful advantage over us."

Joe said to me, "This is a hard thing to say, but do you think she's still alive?"

I wanted to say *I hope so*, but I couldn't make the words come out.

Joe said, "If you was in his place, would you have kept her alive?"

I waited a moment before I said it. "No."

"Keepin' her alive is just one more thing for him to deal with."

Jericho said, "But he needs her to use as a shield. You and Mister Wilson said it yourself."

Sam said, "He only needs us to think she's alive."

"All right," I said. "We go in. And we go in with the sole purpose of killing Conrad. Stopping him. He doesn't go any further."

I gave them each a look in the eye. "I'm activating myself as a Texas Ranger right here and on the spot. And I'm making you all Rangers, as of this very moment. I have that authority. As the lead Ranger, I'm authorizing all of you to shoot him on sight. I'll inform Captain McNelly afterward."

Jericho said, "What if none of us lives through this?"

"Then it'll be our little secret."

41

A SMALL SOD HOUSE STOOD maybe a quarter mile from town. It was so small it was hardly a cabin. It was said a couple of cowhands had attempted to start a ranch here thirty years earlier, and had failed. The roof of the house was made with wood timbers, but they had given way to dry rot and collapsed, and one wall was sagging inward. I doubted it would survive another year. But it seemed to be a good place to leave our horses.

"Will," I said. "You're not gonna like this, but I need you to stay here with the horses."

"You're right. I don't like it. With all due respect, Marshal," he said, "I want to go in and help bring that sum'bitch down."

"I appreciate that. But think about it. If you were in that town in his place and needed to escape, and to do it without any of us seeing who you were, what would you do?"

Will shrugged his shoulders. He wasn't very good at thinking like an outlaw.

Joe said, "I'd wait until you and your deputies made it on foot almost to the town, then I'd back-track you to this place and take the horses with me. Or at least scatter 'em really good. That way you wouldn't be able to follow me."

"Bulls eye." I looked to Will. "I need you to be alert. Keep your rifle ready. If you see anyone coming from town and it's not Maddie or one of us, shoot to kill."

Will said, "Yessir."

The rest of us started toward town. I had a

Winchester in my hands. Sam had an old Henry. Not as efficient as a Winchester, but still a good rifle. Jericho had his sawed-off strapped to his back, and in his hands was another Winchester with a normal-length barrel. Joe had his scattergun.

We also brought along a couple of canteens. The wind was hot in our faces, and occasionally dust would get stirred up, and the sun was harsh overhead. We would need water before we got to the town.

We moved at a fast pace. Not running, because it wouldn't do for us to be worn out when we got there. But we didn't stroll, either.

As we moved along, I said, "I like the idea of the livery barn. The more I think about it, the more I think that's where I would make a stand."

Joe said, "Been thinkin' about that. Another possibility is your office. It sets on the edge of town, facing the street but not connected to either side. Anyone holed up in there would have a good field of fire no matter which way we came."

"That would be my second choice," Sam said. "But I agree with Tremain. My first choice would be the livery barn."

After a time, the town stood ahead of us in the distance. Its buildings looked gray and weatherworn, and they danced in the heat waves.

I pulled the plug from one of the canteens and took a couple of swallows. The water was warm and tasted a little metallic, like it often does from a canteen. But it was wet and on a day like this, wet was all that mattered.

Joe said, "That's the back of Nell's restaurant ahead of us. From the second floor, we might be able to get a good shot at the livery barn."

The livery was across from Nell's and over a little, so from Nell's the barn stood at a right angle.

"Maybe," I said. "But it also limits our field of fire to one side of the building only."

Sam grinned. "You could have been a field general, you know that?"

We continued on, and then eventually came to the alley between Nell's and the building beside it. I was first in line, and stopped at the end of the alley, trying to remain in the shadows as much as possible and still get a look at the livery.

The barn doors were shut tight, as was the hay loft. The door to the loft was tall enough that a man could stand there, if he bent down a little.

Then I noticed something odd. A timber stuck out from the wall just above the loft door, like with most barns, but a rope was tied to this timber and then run in to the loft through the gap between the door and the jamb.

"You think he's in there?" Joe said, sidling up beside me.

"I don't know."

I looked back to Sam. I said, "Sam, you and Joe work your way down the street. Cross at the far end of town and then come up behind the barn. If he tries to get out through the back door, you'll be right there."

Joe said, "Give us twenty minutes."

I nodded, pulling a pocket watch from my vest. "You have it."

Joe and Sam slipped out through the back of the alley.

"He seems to be changing his approach," I said to Jericho. "Up until now, he's been getting the drop on us, one by one. Killing us, and then hanging us after the fact to make a point. But I don't see how he can hope to do that now."

Jericho said, "Maybe he's getting desperate. Or maybe he's changing his approach to try to keep us from getting ahead of him in his thinking. He's hoping to get both you and Maddie at the same time. It kind of makes sense. You and Maddie were both responsible for his arrest. It might make sense to go after both of you at once. And he don't know Doc's still alive. By his reckonin', he'll be getting all three of you today."

I nodded. "And I think I know how to draw him out into the open."

We waited. I looked down at my watch again. Joe and Sam had been gone fourteen minutes.

I said, "Jericho, you said you've killed a man before."

"Yes sir. Didn't like it, but it had to be done. And I can do it again."

Something in his eye told me he could.

I said, "You're the best shot with a rifle I ever seen. I want you to train your rifle on that livery barn. If Conrad shows his face, even for a second, I want you to take his head off. Don't hesitate. Don't wait for instructions. I want you aiming at that livery with a round chambered, ready to fire."

He said, "I won't miss."

I looked down at my watch. Almost time. I took another swallow from the canteen and set it down in the dirt.

The wind blew a small gust of dust along the street. From somewhere down the empty street, a dog barked.

I glanced at my watch. It had been twenty minutes.

"All right," I said. "Let's hope Joe and Sam are in place."

"What if Conrad ain't in the livery?"

"Then we'll go through this town building-by-building until we find him."

Jericho went to the end of the alley, jacked the rifle to chamber a round, and then brought the rifle to his shoulder and aimed it at the livery.

"I'm ready," he said.

"All right. I'm going to go out there and give him something to shoot at."

He lowered his rifle and looked at me. "Marshal?"

"It's the only way to draw him out. Sometimes, being a lawman isn't a job you get out of alive."

He nodded. He didn't like it, but he understood the reality of the situation.

He looked back to the livery and brought the rifle back to his shoulder.

With my pistol in my hand, I stepped out into the street. I called out, "Conrad!"

I waited. All was quiet. I could hear the Texas wind whistling through an alley.

I called out his name again.

And then the hayloft door flew open, and the man I had known as Silas Black stepped into view. And he was holding Maddie in front of him. She was on her feet, but he had a grip on one of her shoulders, and a rope was around her neck. The rope that was attached to the post outside the hay loft door.

"Marshal!" Conrad called down to me. "Throw down that gun, or I give her a push and she dies just like my brother did!"

42

JERICHO STOOD with his rifle pressed against his shoulder and aimed toward the loft, but he held his fire.

He said, "I can't get a clear shot. I'll hit Miss Shannon."

Maddie was still in her green dress. Her hair had come loose and it looked like she had a bruise on her face. It made me want to kill Conrad. Now it had nothing to do with enforcement of the law. Conrad had made it personal.

Her hands were tied behind her back. Her eyes were on me, but I didn't see fear in them. I saw anger.

"Jericho," I called back, but without taking my eyes off Maddie. "Can you shoot that rope?"

Maddie then snapped her head back and into Conrad's face. He staggered back a step, but gave her a push.

She fell from the hay loft, the rope around her neck.

Jericho's rifle fired.

The bullet parted the rope like a knife through butter.

Maddie fell to the street below, hitting the dirt hard. I began charging across the street to her.

Jericho jacked the gun and fired again, trying to get a shot off at Conrad, but Conrad had already backed into the hayloft.

Joe and Sam came running around from the side alley.

Jericho jacked another round into his rifle, and as much as he must have wanted to run out and join us and make sure Maddie was okay, he held his ground and aimed his rifle, waiting for another potential shot at Conrad.

I was the first to her. She was conscious, but shaken up. Her hair and face were smeared with dust.

I landed on my knees in the dirt beside her. "Maddie."

"I'm all right," she said, though she sounded a little shaky. "I think I hurt my ankle, though."

I took her face in my hands. "Did he..?"

She shook her head. "No. I tried to fight him and he knocked me down, but he didn't touch me otherwise."

Joe pulled a hunting knife that was almost as long as a small sword, and cut her wrists free.

Then the barn doors flew open, and out came some horses. Eight it looked like, at first glance. A first glance was all I got. They were charging out in a panic, and we were right in their path.

I dove over Maddie trying to give her cover, and I covered my head with my arms. Sam had run over to make sure Maddie was all right, and Joe was right behind him. The horses ran over all of us.

The leg of one horse caught me in the shoulder and sent me sprawling, and the hoof of another caught me in the ribs. And then they were gone, galloping away down the street.

They had kicked up a cloud of dust all around us. I had landed on my back and rolled to my knees, coughing and squinting my eyes through the cloud. I wasn't sure how badly hurt my ribs were.

My throat felt like sandpaper from the dust, but I choked out the word, "Maddie!"

"I'm all right," she said.

Though her ankle had been hurt in the fall, she was otherwise okay. But Sam was down. She crawled over to him.

I got to my feet and took a staggering step, and evaluated the pain in my rib. I had broken a rib once before, years ago, so I knew what it felt like. I thought this time my rib was probably just bruised.

Maddie said at me. "Sam's unconscious. Looks like a hoof kicked him in the head. He needs a doctor."

"And the only doctor in town is out at the Brimley place, with a bullet in him."

Joe was sitting up, holding his left shoulder. "There's that horse doctor. The one that worked on me when I got my hand all shot up last summer."

Doctor Theophilus Ross. Called Phil by most folks. He was still in town. I generally didn't think of him when I thought of a doctor. Somewhere between fifty and sixty, with a face reddened from too much whiskey over the years. He made living treating horses and cattle in the area, and spent his money in the saloon.

Jericho had come over.

He said, "Ross is out at the Brimley ranch, with everyone else. I saw him there today. I'll ride out and get him."

I thought I smelled smoke. I looked back at the barn, and I could see why the horses had been running.

I said, "The sum'bitch set the barn on fire."

Smoke was pouring out of the open barn doorway like a huge cloud, and I could see flames dancing inside.

Jericho and I managed to drag Sam away from the barn and onto a boardwalk. Maddie couldn't take a step on her leg, so I scooped her up, her dress billowing in my arms, and carried her. Joe was on his feet, though he couldn't move his left arm.

Maddie said, "Austin, we have to do something. Sam needs a doctor."

I had to make a decision. I had to go after Conrad. If we let him get away, then he would be free to strike again. This had to end now. And yet, Sam needed a doctor. If I sent Jericho to ride back to the Brimley place, then the other three would be left here defenseless. Jericho was the only one in any condition to fight.

Joe made the decision for me. He said, "I can't shoot with my right, but I'm on my feet. I can run back to them horses. And I can ride."

I nodded. "Go."

Without even going back to fetch his hat out of the dirt, Joe began away at a light run across the street and away down the alley.

I said to Jericho, "I want you to stay here with the others. If Conrad doubles back for you, kill him. Don't try to arrest him. Don't take any chances."

Jericho nodded.

"Austin," Maddie said. "I don't want you going after him alone."

I said, "I'll be all right."

I gave her a kiss, then reached down to my holster and found my gun wasn't there. A gun is heavy and I should have noticed the weight of it was gone, but I supposed I was too shaken up to have realized it.

I went back to the burning barn. Flames were now rising along the roof and black smoke was reaching up to the sky. The lumber was dry and it was going up fast.

In the dirt in front of the barn door, I found my gun, but it was covered with sand. I shook it out, but I could feel sand grinding as I turned the cylinder. I shook it out some more, but decided not to take any chances on it. Not when my life depended on it. I grabbed the rifle Sam had been carrying and opened the action. It looked operational.

I dropped my revolver on the boardwalk. "I doubt this'll fire. But I'm taking Sam's rifle."

I took one last look at the barn. The flames were rising about five feet above the roof. The way the wind was blowing, sparks would be blown out toward the street behind the barn. But if the wind shifted and brought sparks toward the buildings at either side of it, the whole town could go.

I couldn't think about this now. I had to focus my thoughts on Conrad. He already had at least a five-minute head start on me.

I gripped my rifle, one hand on the action and the other on the fore stock, and ran down the alley alongside the burning barn. The hunt was on.

43

THE DOOR AT THE SIDE OF THE BARN WAS
open. He had set the barn on fire, got the horses
running, and then took off through the back door. If
Sam and Joe had waited by the back door like I had
told them to, they would have caught him. But they
had come running around the front at the sound of
gunfire. Human nature. I probably would have done
the same.

There was a corral out behind the barn, so I
ran the length of it, then ducked out of it through the
fence and crouched behind a water trough that was
positioned near a hitching rail.

I looked at the buildings across the back
street. The gunsmith shop, where Jericho had gotten
his rifle altered. Old Eb's Baptist church. A few
houses.

The only way I was going to find Conrad, this
avenging angel, would be to think like him.

He was a master of strategy. This much was
obvious. Sam had been said I could have been a good
battlefield tactician. Now would be the time to see if
he was right.

The way I saw it, as I crouched behind the
water trough and looked down the dusty street, one
option would have been for him to run across the
street and through an alley, and to head to the low
grassy hills outside of town. Wait for nightfall, then
try to find a horse somewhere.

A second option would be to remain in town.
Lay low and wait for people to return from Brimley's,
and then try to grab a horse.

A third option would be to finish his mission, which was apparently to kill those involved in the hanging of his brother. For all Conrad knew, Doc Benson was dead. This meant only four of us remained. Myself, Sam Wilson, Jericho and Joe. And we were all right here in town. Except for Joe, who had taken off to ride out to Brimley's for the horse doctor. Conrad would have freedom of movement because the town was empty. He would probably not get an opportunity like this again.

I thought that if I was in his place, I would cut to the right and work my way back to the main street, and try to figure out where the rest of the group was. How many had been injured in the little stampede he had created. Maybe come up behind them.

I left the water trough and started off to my right, holding my rifle ready so I could snap off a shot.

I crossed an open expanse of sand to the nearest boardwalk. I moved along, the heels of my riding boots tapping along the boards underfoot, and my spurs making light jingling sounds.

I came to the first alley. I flattened against the wall and peered around the corner. Nothing there but a few empty crates.

Behind this building was the saloon. I worked my way down the alley.

As I did this, a thought occurred to me. The saloon had a second floor, where some of the soiled doves worked their trade. An outside balcony overlooked the street, and I thought a man standing on that balcony might have a view of where this alley opened up to the street.

I moved along the alley slowly, cautiously. If Conrad was on the balcony watching the alley, I didn't want him to see me before I saw him. I moved with my back to the wall, and my rifle held ready.

When I was near the end of the alley, I stepped forward for a look at the balcony, and I saw a man standing there with a rifle to his shoulder. I jumped hard to the side as the rifle fired, and the bullet cut through the air where I had been standing and dug into the dirt in the alley behind me.

I stepped into view and snapped a shot at the alley. My bullet was a little low, tearing into the wooden railing, and I saw the man leap away.

I hadn't been able to get a good look at him. I saw he was wearing a wide-brimmed hat and his shirt was dark, but that was all. It was probably Conrad. I couldn't imagine who else it could be. Unless—and this thought occurred to me for the first time—he had someone else working with him.

We should have thought of this sooner. Doc, Joe and me. We had tried to think this situation through as thoroughly as we could, but the possibility that he could have an accomplice never occurred to us, but now seemed so obvious.

I decided I would kick myself for this later. After I had taken care of Conrad.

I chambered a round, and with my back flattened against the wall, I slid down the alley until I was directly beneath the balcony. I then fired up and into the balcony floor, then jacked in another round and fired again, then sent a third bullet through the wood.

The outer door of the saloon was shut and I

presumed it was locked. I wasn't going to waste any time trying the door handle to find out. With another round chambered, I raised a foot and drove my boot through the door. It flew open, part of the door jamb splintering away. The town would have to pay for a new one.

I stepped in, rifle ready.

The bar was to one side. Tables to another. All good places to shoot from. But there were no shots fired at me. The room was quiet and empty.

I crossed the floor, rifle held ready.

I knew he had to be in here. The only other doorway out was in the alley I had just crossed, and it opened up behind the bar. He couldn't have left without me seeing him.

I thought of calling out his name, but decided that would be useless. It would do me no good, and would give him my exact location.

I walked among the tables. There were eight of them, all with chairs turned upside down on top of them. I was ready should he be waiting behind one, but he wasn't here. I checked behind the bar, and found nothing. This meant he was still upstairs.

Had I hit him when I fired? Possibly. But I wasn't going to take any chances. Conrad was one of the most dangerous opponents I had ever faced. In some ways, even more so than his brother was. To make one mistake could cost me my life. And if he got past me, he would be going for the others.

With my rifle held ready, I started up the stairs, taking one step at a time.

I was careful to set my feet down at the end of the step nearest the wall, where the boards would be less likely to creak under my weight. But they did creak a little. These buildings had been put up quickly and the nails slid a bit when you stepped down, creating a little squeaking sound.

There was a small balcony overlooking the barroom below. I remembered Milt the bartender saying the railing was wobbly, again from the place being slapped together so quickly. Milt figured sooner or later, in the brawls that sometimes developed on a Saturday night, it was going to break away and someone was going to crash to the floor below. He had said he planned to fix it one of these days.

I was near the top of the steps when Conrad charged at me. He was in a dark shirt and a wide-brimmed hat. It was apparently Conrad that I had seen on the balcony outside. He came running at full speed and dove at me. I was knocked backward, and fell and went down a couple of steps on my back. My rifle went off and then fell away from me.

Conrad had run down the stairs behind me, and leaped onto me. He tried to push his pistol into my face. He still had the Silas Black beard, but his eyes were crazed.

I was lying upside down on the stairs with Conrad on top of me, and I raised one knee and Conrad was knocked up over my head and away. He rolled headfirst down the stairs. His pistol had been cocked and it went off, the bullet burying itself in a wall.

I got to my feet and charged down the stairs after him. He was only partially to his feet, and I kicked out with one foot and caught his gun hand, and knocked the pistol from his grip.

He then tackled me, and we fell onto the barroom floor grappling with each other. First he was on top, then I was. We rolled into a table and the chairs came crashing down onto us. This bruised us both up a little, but not enough to stop either of us.

We broke away from each other and sprang to our feet.

I drove a fist into his stomach, but was met by solid muscle. His hair and beard were gray, but he was no old man. As Silas Black, he had walked with a cane and talked about a leg wound he received in the war. But he really had no bad leg.

He launched a right cross at me and rocked my head back. He drove a knee up between my legs, but such a thing is not as sure-fired a way to win a fight as you might think. I twisted to one side and his foot caught me on the inside of my leg, just above my knee.

I then stepped in and threw a punch at his face. He raised an arm to block the punch, but I was already coming in with an uppercut, and he couldn't move fast enough and it caught him under the chin. He staggered back a bit.

He glanced about quickly, probably looking for his pistol.

"Give it up," I said. "You're under arrest."

He then charged away from me, and began running up the stairs. I ran after him, and took the stairs two at a time, about five feet behind him the entire way.

He had fired at me with a rifle from the balcony, but had come downstairs with a pistol only. He must have been going to get his rifle, but I wasn't going to give him the chance to use it.

He turned on me, and swung a fist that I was barely able to duck. He then turned again to run into one of the rooms, but I grabbed him by the shirt collar and pulled him back.

He turned toward me and tackled me again, and the momentum carried us both back toward the railing.

I tried to turn us away, but I couldn't. We hit the railing and it gave under our weight, and we crashed onto an empty table below. The table broke, and we fell through it to the floor.

We laid there for a few seconds. I didn't know about him, but I needed to catch my wind and make sure I hadn't broken any bones.

He got to his feet first, but he was hobbling. I pushed to my feet, finding a shoulder felt a little numb. I could barely move my arm.

He was no longer trying to get to the steps, but was making his way to a point a little further down the bar. He had a hand on the bar and was sort of dragging one leg.

Then I saw what he was going for. He had found where his pistol had landed. But I saw my rifle, and as he reached for his gun, I scooped up the Henry and went to jack another round into the chamber.

Except the lever got stuck in mid-motion. Must have been sand caught in the action. The rifle was jammed.

Conrad now had his revolver in his hand, and was aiming it at me.

He said, "I'm afraid I'm not under arrest, Marshal. I feel I should apologize to the memory of my brother, because I surely wanted to get a noose around your neck. I'll just have to settle for shooting you down like the dog you are."

Then, Maddie called out from the doorway, "Conrad! Drop that gun!"

She was standing in her green, checkered dress that was now dusty and torn. On one cheekbone was the bruise she had gotten from tussling with Conrad. But in her other hand was a revolver and she held it steady, and the hammer was hauled back. One thing about Maddie—she could shoot. And she was more than willing to.

But he just grinned. He didn't know her or what she was capable of.

"Miss Shannon," he said, "Put that pistol down or I'll put a bullet in both of you."

I said to him, "You'll never get off the shot. Throw your gun down."

He moved quickly. I'll give him that. He was very skilled at what he did. He probably moved a little slower than he normally would have because of his bum leg, but I don't think it would have made much of a difference. Maddie's gun went off before Conrad could even fire.

The bullet caught him in the forehead, snapping his head backwards. He landed on his back on the beer-stained saloon floor. Maddie stood with her gun hand steady, and already had the pistol cocked again before Conrad had gone fully down.

He had to be dead, I figured, but I knelt by him just to make sure. With men like Conrad and Hooper, you could never be too sure. But there was clearly a bullet hole in his forehead, and his eyes were staring toward the ceiling but no longer seeing. He was about as dead as you could be.

I looked at Maddie and said it. "He's dead."

She lowered her gun, and reached one hand out to the door jamb to brace herself. She was standing on her bad ankle, but barely.

I rested my jammed-up rifle on a table, and then went to her. I wrapped my arms around her and she placed her head against my shoulder. We were both covered with sweat and dust, and were battered and bruised.

"Not the way I imagined this day turning out," I said. "But I think it's over. The Hooper legacy is finally over."

She said, "I want to marry you. Right now. We could have both died today. I don't want to wait anymore. No more big ceremony. I don't care what Mother says. I want to be married right now."

44

THERE WASN'T a big showing at the burial. I didn't expect there to be. Jericho and Will dug the grave, not getting it quite to the standard dimensions of six by six by three, but close enough for government work.

I had never been afraid of work, but my shoulder had been dislocated in the fall from the saloon balcony. Even with it fixed I still couldn't move it very well, and Joe was too banged up from being run over by a horse. And Sam was recovering from being kicked in the head when we were all trampled, but it would be a while before he was fully on his feet. As such, it was up to Jericho and Will to do the digging.

The body was wrapped in a sheet of canvas, just like with his brother. The town didn't want to spend the money slapping together a pine box. I couldn't really find fault with that.

I was in jeans and a white boiled shirt, with my tin star pinned in place. Beside it was my Ranger badge. My gun was at my side and my hat was pulled down tight to keep the Texas wind from lifting it off.

Maddie was beside me. She was also in jeans and had a gun buckled about her hips. She wore a range shirt and somehow looked as elegant in it as most women did in an evening gown. Her hair was pulled back into a long braid. She was using a cane because her ankle was still a little banged up.

Joe was there. And Artie Manchester, one of the deacons of the Baptist Church. He had been filling in at the pulpit while the congregation searched for a replacement for Eb.

Once the grave was dug, Artie said, "Any last words?"

I said, "Cover him over."

Maddie said, "Amen."

Artie thought we were awful.

He said, "He may have done evil things, but he was a child of God, as are we all. It's not for us to judge."

Jericho looked at me and shrugged, and I said, "Cover him over."

He and Will dropped the body into the ground and covered it over with dirt.

When they were finished, I stood looking at the grave. Jericho held a shovel upright and stood leaning on it. Sweat had soaked his shirt and his hair was wet with it. On the ground behind him was his jacket and his sawed-off. Will stood beside him, chugging water from a canteen.

Normally you paid your respects and then left before the grave was covered over, but since this was the brother of Jonathan Hooper, you wanted to see the grave filled in. Not that any of us really thought he could be a threat any longer, it was just that seeing the grave covered over, one shovelful of dirt after another, sort of gave a sense of completion.

I had sent a wire to Captain McNelly to tell him about Ambrose Conrad catching a bullet, and he wired back that he was sending a Ranger out to get my report. Turns out that legally, since I was still officially a Ranger, my dealing with Conrad fell under Ranger jurisdiction. Conrad was wanted in a number of states for various murders, and even a country in South American was after him. All of that would be dealt with at the federal level, but it first had to go through Captain McNelly's office.

Ike Hawkins was the Ranger that McNelly sent out, and he came riding up while we were standing by Conrad's grave.

"Come to pay your respects?" I said, extending my hand.

Hawkins grinned and shook my hand. "Come to get your report. And maybe a glass or two of whiskey. Young Billy said you'd be here."

"Doesn't seem right, in a way," Artie said. "A man is dead. Something should have been said over his grave. A prayer. Something."

I shook my head. "I believe in the Good Lord. But sometimes, there are just some men who need to be killed."

Joe said, in his tight-lipped way, "Couldn't have put it better myself."

Artie gave me a look that said he thought we were terrible. But it wouldn't have seemed right to get all sentimental and religious over a man who seemed to live just to cause death.

I slapped Hawkins on the shoulder. "Come on. Let's go get that whiskey."

45

WE TOOK a table. Maddie joined Hawkins and me in a glass of bourbon. Joe had a tall, foamy beer. Jericho set the sheath holding his sawed-off rifle onto the table, and joined Joe in a beer. Jericho wasn't quite twenty and had a ways to go before he hit drinking age. But I figured he did a man's work and was turning into quite a deputy, so if he wanted a beer, I saw no harm in it.

We were all kind of quiet for a while. Just sitting together, thinking about all that had happened. Then conversation started up. Talk of the weather. Talk of the town. The livery barn had burned to the ground but managed not to take any other buildings with it, and there was going to be a barn-raising in a couple of days.

Hawkins said, "I hear Doc Benson got himself near killed."

I nodded. "Shot and hanged. Both."

Hawkins shook his head. "That kind of thing can ruin your day."

"Looks like he's gonna pull through, though."

The talk shifted to others Conrad had attacked, who hadn't been as lucky as Doc. Victims like Eb Crumby.

The Baptists were searching for a replacement for him, but the Methodists had an even deeper concern than that.

"Turns out there was a real Silas Black," I said. "A few days ago, I sent a wire off to the Methodist organization back east, the one our church is hooked up with. There was actually a Methodist minister by that name. He had been assigned to our church, but was way-laid along the way. His body was found in an alley in Ohio, but they couldn't identify it for a while. Just a week ago, someone from the organization identified the body by a ring the real Reverend Black had worn."

Conrad had apparently been the killer, and it was ironically the real Reverend Black's credentials on the wall in the pastor's office at the church.

I said, "While Conrad was here masquerading as the Reverend Black, he performed three baptisms and a wedding. All this is going to have to be done over, once they find a legitimate minister. Meanwhile, the young couple had settled into a sod house. They're planning to build a farm. But they had been unknowingly living in sin for the past few weeks. The poor girl has moved back in with her parents while they wait for a new minister."

Hawkins was laughing and stamping one foot on the floor.

"That's not funny," Maddie said, but she was grinning and soon was laughing. Then we all were.

"Speakin' of nuptials," Hawkins said, glancing from Maddie to me, "I heard you two are fixin' to tie the knot."

I nodded. I was hit once again with what had been bothering me. The fact that Maddie was much more wealthy than I had originally realized last summer, and I owned little more than the clothes on my back.

I tried not to let it show. I said to Hawkins, "That's right."

"The sooner the better," Maddie said.

"There's no minister in town at the moment, and Mister Garret was the only Justice of the Peace. But we're going to have a wedding as soon as we can."

Hawkins said, "Well, turns out I'm a Justice of the Peace."

We all looked at him.

He said, "It ain't that hard to do. You just fill out a few papers and pay a small fee. I figured it'd be a wise thing to do. Captain McNelly sometimes sends me to far-reaching parts of Texas, where I'm the only law present. The Rangers have a lot of authority, but it doesn't hurt to be a Justice of the Peace, too."

Maddie said, "Would you like to perform a wedding?"

"Well, I've gotta head back tomorrow."

She looked at me and smiled. "This afternoon is fine with me."

I smiled. It was genuine. I couldn't not smile when she turned hers on me.

I said, "Miss Shannon, you have yourself a wedding date."

46

THERE WAS a lot to do. A wedding was going to be held in just a few hours. It seemed like my life suddenly exploded into a flurry of activity.

It was still a few days before my next pay day, but the general store loaned me some clothes. Within three hours, I was at the ranch wearing a white boiled shirt, the dark jacket Doc had loaned me for dinner at the ranch, a checkered vest and a scarf-like thing that sort of folded over on itself in front of me. I had never seen such a thing before. Doc called it a *cravat*.

Joe was there. He was in a jacket and had trimmed down his juniper bush of a beard, and managed a string tie. He was to be my best man.

Nell was there, too. After we decided on the afternoon wedding, Maddie had run down the street to the restaurant to ask Nell to be her maid of honor. Nell had said yes, and the two squealed and hugged the way women do when they plan weddings.

Joe and I were at the ranch by one in the afternoon. We were standing on the front porch with Sam and we each were working on a cigar, when Maddie stepped out. The wedding was still an hour away, and she had just had a bath and was in a robe and her hair was all wrapped up in a towel.

"Hey," Joe said, "don't you know it's bad luck to let the groom see you before the wedding?"

"Joe," she said. "He saw me just this morning."

"Oh, yeah."

Sam was chuckling.

"So," I said to her. "I know your mother must be about as against this as a body can be."

"She'll be on her best behavior," Maddie said. "I can promise you that."

I wouldn't have wanted to be in the room when Maddie and her mother had that discussion.

Maddie touched my arm. "Austin, can we talk for a minute?"

Sam and Joe excused themselves.

She said, "Austin, you want this wedding, don't you?"

I set the cigar down on the porch railing, and took Maddie gently by the shoulders. "Of course I do."

"Something's been troubling you. It has for weeks now."

"No," I said. "I'm fine. Just the pressures of the job. The whole mess with Conrad."

She shook her head. "It's more than that. I can see it weighing on you right now."

I hadn't wanted to tell her. I didn't really know how. But now I decided to just say it, so I did. I told her what her mother had said to me, but I had been having thoughts in that direction on my own even before.

She shook her head. "My mother. There's no end to her reach, is there?"

I said, "I'm sure she means well."

"No, she doesn't. She seldom does."

Maddie turned away and started pacing. She held one hand across her chest to her shoulder so the Texas wind wouldn't whip her robe open. Her other hand was gripped around the handle of a cane.

She said, "I've had to face the truth about Mother. I had to do this long ago. I've learned to live with it, more or less. While I knew Father loved me and was everything a father could be, and Sam is here and is like a father to me, Mother lives for herself only. When she talks about wanting something for someone's own good, what she means is she is trying to manipulate a situation for her own good."

"Maddie..," I said, not really knowing what to say. I couldn't imagine saying those words about my own mother.

She turned to me. "No, it's all right. I've come to accept her for what she is. This is why I'm my father's daughter, and always have been. I made a decision long ago, when I was just a child, that I was going to be the apple that didn't fall far from his tree, not hers."

She placed a hand gently along the side of my face. "The money means nothing to me. What we have isn't about money. I know you don't care about it. You've never lived your life like you did. A man as capable as you are could have been as rich as Mother by now, if you had wanted to be. The fact that you don't is one of the things I love about you."

"I'm a lawman," I said. "Not a rancher."

"I don't see any reason why I can't run the ranch, and you continue to wear the badge."

I felt like the weight was falling from my shoulders. Maybe I should have talked to her about this earlier.

I said, "Where will we live? After all, I can't be too far from town. I need to be nearby, should someone need the marshal. But I can't see you sharing that little bunk with me in the corner of my office."

"We'll figure that out, later. But tonight, I want us to ride back out to our little line shack. It can serve as our honeymoon cabin."

I nodded. I realized I was smiling. "Joe and Jericho can handle things in town for a few days."

Our lips met and then she was in my arms, and her towel fell from her head and my fingers were running through her wet hair.

We didn't hear the door open, but we heard Joe say, "I thought you weren't supposed to kiss the bride until after the ceremony."

47

I STOOD in front of the great stone hearth in the parlor of the Shannon Ranch house. Joe was beside me. Ike Hawkins was there, a Bible in one hand. The Bible wasn't his—he had borrowed that from Doc. He also had been given a white shirt and a black string tie from a clothing store in town. I reassured the store owner he would be reimbursed by the Texas Rangers.

Turned out Clem, the cowhand who had driven Maddie and me out to the line cabin the day she arrived in town, was a fair hand at a banjo. You've never heard anything until you've heard the wedding march played on a banjo. We had put this wedding together on short notice, so Clem sat on a wooden upright chair, and with a banjo on his knee, started plucking out the strains of the march.

First Nell stepped out, as the matron-of-honor. Maddie had explained to me it was *matron* and not *maid* because even though Nell was young and unmarried, she was actually a widow.

The men from the ranch and some folks from town were gathered in the parlor and parted to form an aisle for Nell to walk down. Amelia was present, standing there in quiet misery.

Nell walked through as Clem plucked away on the banjo, and took her place at the other side of Hawkins.

Maddie then stepped out from the kitchen. She was in a gown she had brought with her from St. Louis. A gown I hadn't seen. It was a deep blue color, the neckline falling gently off the shoulders. Her hair was up in a tangle of waves and curls, somehow being held into place.

She gave me a look that took my breath away. A smile, but it was more the look in her eyes. Warm. Loving. Happy.

Sam was with her, standing in the place of her father. He would be giving her away. It seemed fitting—Sam was now the closest thing to a father she had.

With the banjo plucking out the notes to the wedding march, she and Sam walked up to me. They moved along a little slowly because of Maddie's ankle, but she wanted to walk down the aisle without her cane.

They approached the hearth, and then she stood before me and Sam stepped back.

I had no ring to give her, but Nell had come through in a pinch, giving me a treasure from her family that I didn't feel worthy to accept. The wedding ring her grandmother had worn.

I had said to Nell, "I can't accept this."

She had said, "I would be honored if you would. You're a good man, and Maddie has become a good friend."

And so, I stood with Nell's grandmother's wedding ring in my jacket pocket.

"Well," Hawkins said. "I ain't never been much on words, and I ain't never done a wedding before."

Amelia rolled her eyes.

Hawkins said, "I won't pretend to know much about the Good Book. I believe in the Almighty, but I never done much reading of his Word. But I'll say this. I seen the way this here gal looked at Tremain just now, when she come out of the kitchen. And I seen the way Tremain was looking at her. You ain't gonna find truer love than that."

Joe muttered an, "Amen."

Hawkins said, "Maddie, what's your full name?"

Maddie said, "Madelyn Amelia Ariana Shannon."

"My, that's pretty. All right, Madelyn Amelia Ariana Shannon, will you promise to do good by this here feller. Treat him good. Don't never cheat on him. Be there when he's hurtin' and be there when he's not. Love him forever."

She was looking at me with a broad smile and a glint of moisture in her eyes. "Always."

'And you, Tremain. Austin Tremain. What's yer middle name?"

I grinned and a couple of people chuckled.

I said, "Mordecai."

He gave me a look like he didn't quite believe me. "Mordecai? Really?"

I shrugged. "It was my grandfather's name."

Amelia was shaking her head and muttering something. I suppose she had always planned to have practically a royal wedding for her daughter. This wedding was probably like something out of a nightmare for her. What she didn't realize—maybe she wasn't capable of it—was that while this ceremony wasn't fancy, it was filled with feeling. With heart. With love.

Hawkins said, "Austin Mordecai Tremain, do you take this here gal to be your wife? To love her always? Always be there for her? Take care of her always? Never take no other. To have and to hold and all that?"

I was looking into Maddie's eyes. "And all that. I do."

"Then, by the power granted me by the glorious Republic of Texas, I pronounce you two husband and wife."

He didn't have to tell me to kiss the bride.

Afterward, refreshments were served. Amelia had made up some of those hor's doerves things she liked so much. I made my way out to the porch for a little fresh air. In one hand I had a glass of bourbon.

I wasn't aware Amelia had followed me until she said from the open doorway behind me, "I suppose congratulations are in order."

I mistakenly thought she was being polite, maybe trying to create some good will between us. I gave a polite smile and said, "It would seem so."

"Well, you won't get any from me." She stepped fully onto the porch. I now saw that she wasn't being gracious, but gearing up for war.

She said, "You kept the money I gave you. I was paying you to leave. You kept the money but you're still here. I know you think you're being cute, considering it an endowment for the town."

"Mrs. Shannon," I said, trying to figure what to say to this woman. I finally decided to just say it. "I don't want a war. But I'm here. I'm in your daughter's life. You and I have to learn to tolerate each other."

"I know you think you have won, Marshal.

My daughter now wears your ring. But I want to assure you that you haven't won. Believe me, you are incapable of playing the game on my level."

I wasn't quite sure what she was talking about. I said, "Are you threatening me?"

"I'm saying that you will not inherit a cent of the family money. I fully intend that you will not be around long enough to. One way or another, you are going away. There are no limits—there is no line I won't cross. Not when the stakes are this high. Not when you are trifling with my family."

She glared at me. It was like looking into the eyes of a rattler that was about to strike. I had faced down more than one gunfighter, more than one outlaw, but I never saw any with eyes more deadly than those of Amelia McAllister Shannon.

She turned and strode away, through the doorway and back into the parlor. Sam was stepping out onto the porch and she almost ran him over.

"Well," he said. "That was almost the second time this week I was trampled."

Sam had a glass of bourbon in one hand and a cigar in the other, and he looked over his shoulder as Amelia stormed away, driving her heels into the floorboards.

"What was that all about?" he asked.

I told him. No point in not doing so.

He listened silently, taking an occasional draft of smoke from his cigar.

I then said, "You don't seem surprised by any of this."

He said, "I've known her a long time. No, I'm not surprised."

"She's trying to scare me away."

"Yeah, that she is. But be aware, that woman don't bluff. I've come to believe she's capable of anything."

"What about Maddie? How do I tell her this? How do I tell her that her own mother all but threatened to kill me?"

Sam drew in some smoke, held it thoughtfully for a moment, then let it out slowly.

"You don't."

I didn't like the sound of that.

I said, "I don't want to have any secrets from her. My mother and father had the kind of marriage where they never had any secrets. That's the kind of marriage I want with Maddie."

Sam looked at me. "That's a good thing. And yet, there are some things that just can't be said. Believe me, I know. There are some truths that would just cause more harm than good. The pain you might feel in not telling her would be less than the pain it might cause her to know."

There was something about the way Sam was saying what he said that told me he had experience with it. I didn't know how to ask him, so I didn't.

I said, "I sure don't want to cause her pain."

Sam let his gaze wander out to the low, grassy hills beyond the barn. "So, you live with it. At least for now. A truth like that might have to come out some day. But there's no need for it to do so until it has to."

He took another puff on the cigar. "And besides, Amelia's heading back to St. Louie in a few days. Maybe she'll stay there. The less time she spends here, the less harm she can do."

"Let's hope."

48

I WENT to visit Doc. He couldn't be at the wedding because he had taken a bullet and been hanged. I figured that was a good enough reason.

He was renting the top floor of the feed store. The front part was his office and the back part was where he lived. This was where I found him.

His living quarters consisted of two rooms. One he used for a parlor, and the other for a bedroom. He had no kitchen and took all of his meals at Nell's. There was a small wood stove that he used to keep himself warm when the Texas night got cold, and to brew an occasional pot of coffee.

I found him stretched out on a sofa. He was in a night shirt and a robe.

"Sorry I couldn't be at the wedding," he said. "Getting hanged and shot seems to have a way of taking the sand out of a man."

He was still speaking a little hoarsely, and there was a strong rope burn around his neck.

I said, "I figure once you're on your feet, Maddie and I will let you buy us dinner and we'll call it even."

He grinned. "Mighty generous of you."

I didn't wait to be invited to sit down. Such civilized pleasantries were necessary when a woman was present, but when it was only men in the room, we just sat down.

There was an old Queen Anne's chair that didn't match the sofa. The chair had faded purple velvet upholstery, and the sofa was tattered. I think it might have been brown once. Now it was the color of the desert in the evening. I took the chair.

I tossed my hat onto a small coffee table that stood between the chair and the sofa. The night was getting a little chilly so I was wearing a canvas jacket, but now that I was inside and Doc had a fire going in the stove, I decided to unbutton the jacket.

"I just wanted to make sure you were all right," I said.

"It's painful," he said. "The bullet wound. I'm lucky that he was using a derringer. My ribs caught the bullet and I lost a lot of blood. If it had been a full-sized pistol, the bullet would have done a lot more damage than it did. And my throat hurts. But I'll be all right."

"Taking anything for the pain?"

He shook his head. "I could prescribe myself some laudanum or morphine. But I don't like to use it. I've seen people become addicted to that stuff. I hate to prescribe it."

"I suppose anything that numbs pain is going to carry that risk."

He nodded gravely. "All too true."

"But some are more pleasant than others." I reached into my jacket and pulled out a pint of bourbon. "I just filled this prescription at the saloon."

He gave a grin. "Well, doctor, there are two glasses in the cupboard over there."

He had a small corner hutch that was scratched up. His entire parlor set was mix-and-match. On the frontier, money was scarce and resources were few, so you often took what you could find.

I got the glasses and pulled the cork on the

bourbon and poured two glasses and handed one to Doc.

Doc knocked back a mouthful, and I watched his face as it burned its way down.

He said, "That was a little painful. Maybe this isn't such a good idea, so soon after being hanged."

"You know a lot, Doc. You know a lot more than I do about the more sophisticated side of life. But no one has ever shown you how to drink whiskey."

So I gave him the lesson the old scout had given me. I watched as Doc took an ounce back on his tongue, holding his breath while he did so, then swallowed and slowly exhaled.

"Oh, that's nice," he said. "And it didn't burn."

I took a drink from my own glass.

I had noticed that Doc's smile seemed a little half-hearted. At first I thought it was because of the bullet and the hanging, but now I was starting to wonder.

I said, "Doc, something's wrong. Out with it."

He let out a long, tired sigh, and said, "I can't believe I let him get the jump on me. Conrad. I really believed no man could get the jump on me."

I said, "I've figured there's a lot more to you than being a doctor. You didn't just learn how to fight during the War."

He shook his head. "I'll tell you the whole story sometime."

I took another belt of bourbon. "Doc, have you figured out who Joe is?"

He shrugged. "Joe Smith, I suppose."

"There's a lot more to him, too. That's for him to tell. But I can tell you this. He's one of the most formidable men I've ever met. Between you and me and him, I would put my money on him every time. But no man is perfect. Every man can be jumped. Even Joe."

He nodded. "I guess I learned that lesson the hard way."

"The fact that he was able to get the jump on you tells me just how good he actually was."

"Well, I thank you for that." He took another drink of bourbon. "I was just coming out of my office and about to head down the stairs."

Doc's office had a flight of wooden stairs outside that took you down to the boardwalk in front of the feed store.

Doc said, "He was there. Conrad. Passing himself off as Silas Black. He was walking with a cane, an injury he claimed he attained in the War. I believed him. Even though I'm a medical man, his limp was very convincing. He told me young Billy had gotten himself stepped on by a horse again and injured his foot. Easy to believe. I followed him down to Nell's, where he said Billy was. The street was otherwise empty, because everyone was out at the barn dance, already. Then he turned, derringer in hand, and just shot me."

Doc drew a breath. "I fell backward. Hit my head on something, I suppose. I don't really remember what. I blacked out and when I woke up, I was at the Brimley place, in the parlor. He had a rope around my neck and was hoisting me up. I know a few things about human anatomy, and I knew as long as my neck didn't break, I could tighten up my neck muscles and hang there. But I had to let him think I was still unconscious so he wouldn't shoot me again, or stick a knife into me.

"The thing is, it's hard to breathe when you're hanging like that. I was about to black out again when you and the others came in."

"Well, Doc, I'm just glad we got there when we did."

He shrugged and gave a half-hearted smirk. "Some deputy I turned out to be."

"Did I ever tell you about the time I got myself caught by the Apaches? Back when I was a scout. I thought I was good enough not to allow that to happen, but it did. If it wasn't for that old scout, I wouldn't be here to tell you about it."

"The same scout who showed you how to drink whiskey?"

I nodded. "His name was Apache Jim Layton."

And Doc and I sat there and drank whiskey, and I told him how old Jim Layton had saved me from the Apaches, after my own carelessness had let me get captured in the first place. And somewhere in all of that, as the Texas winds blew against the wall outside and rattled the panes in his windows, the half-heartedness left Doc's grin, and he became more like himself again.

49

A WEEK LATER, IT WAS time for Amelia to head back St. Louis. Not a moment too soon, if you asked me. Maddie helped her mother pack up her trunks and valises, and we all escorted her to town.

Maddie's cane was now gone. She was in her range shirt and jeans, with her gun buckled about her hips. I'm sure Amelia would have liked to fuss about this, but was learning not to bother.

In front of the waiting stagecoach, Amelia gave her daughter an embrace, but it wasn't a heart-felt hug of love. It was a gentle sort of listless little embrace.

"Take care, my darling daughter," Amelia said.

"You too, Mother."

Amelia looked at me. I looked at her. Neither of us said anything. She had already declared where she stood on the subject of Maddie and me. There was nothing more to be said.

Amelia turned to step into the coach. Hank offered a hand, and she took it but never actually looked at him. I had noticed she never actually looked at someone she thought was beneath her. She looked through them, or beyond them, but never quite at them.

Julio the Italian climbed up onto the stage to ride with Hank. I reached a hand up to Julio, and he grasped it. I said to him, "Be well, my friend."

"I will," he said in perfect English. "You be well, too. Wearing the badge is a dangerous job."

"I wouldn't trade with you."

He laughed.

Amelia called from inside the coach, "Julio, are my bags all loaded?"

"Si, Senora," he called back, his broken English returning. "We ready to leave."

The driver called out a *giddyap*, and the stage rolled on its way.

Maddie and I had decided to spend every other night out at the ranch. When we weren't there, we stayed in town.

Since my pay was actually less than a local cowhand earned, the town business leaders compensated in various ways such as free meals at Nell's and free ammunition from the gunsmith. One way the hotel owner compensated was to let Maddie and me have a room permanently.

When we weren't in town, I knew everything would be all right. Joe was as capable as a man could be, and I knew the town was in good hands. Jericho was there too, and he was turning into a good man and a fine lawman.

Joe and Jericho were now full-time deputies. I was paying them from the endowment I received from Amelia. That wad of cash wouldn't last forever, but when it was gone, I would figure out something. One thing I had learned over the years was to let tomorrow take care of tomorrow's worries.

Tonight was to be one of Maddie's and my nights in town. It was pay day for the ranches in the area, which meant tonight was going to be a wild one.

It was late afternoon as Maddie and I were

sitting in my office with a cup of coffee. Cowhands had begun drifting in, but the town was still quiet. Things generally didn't heat up until after dark.

As we sat drinking coffee, I thought about the threat Amelia had given me. And I thought about how uncomfortable I was not telling Maddie about it. I didn't want to keep secrets from her. But I also thought about what Sam said. Sometimes certain things have to be told at the right time.

My cup was empty and I thought about refilling it. The stove was cold—this coffee had come from Nell. I was about to ask Maddie if she wanted to walk with me down to Nell's, when we heard a woman scream and some glass shattering. Sounded like a window being smashed in. The last time I had heard a sound like this, one cowhand had thrown another through the saloon window.

"It's starting early," I said, getting to my feet. The coffee would have to wait. "I've gotta go to work."

Maddie smiled. "I'll be here waiting."

I stepped outside and crossed the expanse of open street between my office and the nearest boardwalk. Jericho came running toward me.

"You hear that?" he said. "Came from the saloon."

"Let's go restore some law-and-order," I said.

Jericho fell into place beside me and we strode down the boardwalk toward the saloon.

21950915R00153

Printed in Poland
by Amazon Fulfillment
Poland Sp. z o.o., Wrocław